"Wright's Wrath has voice, character, charm - and most importantly a mystery that will have you holding your breath until the very end. You won't want to put it down!"
October K Santerelli

For April
*No one has to put up with my nonsense more than you, and
you still find it in your heart to listen and urge me forward.*

In Memory of David Farland.
*When I write, I hear your words softly correcting me and
prompting me to add more.*

DEATH'S CONTRACT

BOOK TWO OF THE KHIMMER CHRONICLES

KEVIN A DAVIS

Inkd
Publishing

CONTENTS

DEATH'S CONTRACT

This is the second book in the Khimmer Chronicles series. It centers around Ahnjii and Khimmer, the mind of her adaptive Nightarmor.

Ahnjii meets the Upre in this novel, particularly one who won't take no for an answer. She is still trying to navigate a new world, and still making mistakes.

"DARK GODDESS, YES." I pushed myself off the sweaty, hairy wildling and slapped his enlarged chest.

"Ahnjii!" He called out my name, though I couldn't remember his.

I'd picked him up at a local wildling bar and had come back to his place without saying his name once. He smelled musky mixed with an inhuman scent that reminded me of coffee or chocolate. His tough fur retracted as he shifted back to a human form.

"That was fun." I wiped sweat off my face and jerked my head toward his front door. "It's late."

He grunted and yawned, not as drunk as when we'd walked to his house. "You could stay." His voice still had a deep tone, like grating gravel. Sprawled on his couch, he made no sign of getting up. Long black hair and bronze skin made up his handsome human form, sweat glistened on his chest from our tussle, and his eyes had glints of red remaining from the shifting.

"Thanks." I touched the small scratch he'd left on my back before I retrieved my scattered pile of clothes on the floor. My braid had loosened and fuzzed during our antics, itching at my neck. "Maybe another time. Need to feed Woo." I'd likely never be back again. If wildlings were anything like other men, they got a little possessive once you had sex; it became worse if you did them more than once. I'd gotten the curiosity out of my system. We'd taken precautions, even though wildlings supposedly weren't susceptible to human sexual diseases; I didn't need a half wildling, half human baby.

When I stepped outside, I shivered in the frigid air. The breeze carried the pervasive fumes of exhaust and sharp putrid notes of garbage. The sound of traffic was distant on these quiet streets. I'd realized wildling neighborhoods were muted, though they did drive cars. The stars were rare above this part of Tallahassee, hidden by the city lights even with few porch lamps lit. Shadows hung between short block houses and stretched into the street.

Anybody watching? I thought to Khimmer, the mind of Nightarmor.

I do not believe so, Mistress. No one close is outside or at their windows.

Try that hoodie again. It's cold. My friend Tyler named the Earth month as February and said it would be warming soon. Earlier, I'd opted for my usual tank top and jean shorts. The night had turned exceptionally chilly.

Nightarmor poured across my body from its bangles, arm bands, belt, and choker to form a short cloak of flexible, soft metal with a cowl and long sleeves. It cut the breeze as I crossed through College Town and began to jog toward my apartment. There was still activity at this time of the morning.

The student apartments along my street were multiple tall buildings of the same design. On my right, one had a party blaring out an open door on the third floor. A cluster of college kids leaned on cars in the parking lot, laughing and drinking as I jogged past. The road darkened ahead where my apartment waited.

Mrs. Forster's pink flamingos dotted the patches of withered grass and glowed under the street lamp. At least she'd be asleep at this hour. The smell of the nearby water added a stagnant reek to the chill air. I took the stairs two at a time, key already in hand. Earth's crescent moon lit the gray peeling walls of my apartment; it was still a strange sight even after ten months.

Woo whistled from the bathroom as I closed the front door and locked it.

Remove hoodie.

Yes, Mistress.

Nightarmor melted off to my choker, arm bands, and bangles. Heat flowed from the vent in the middle of my barren apartment. I needed to buy a couple chairs at least.

"Miss me, Woo?" I shoved the key in my front pocket and started taking my shorts off as I walked to the archway that led to my bathroom, bedroom, and an empty storage closet.

Woo slept on the shower curtain rod when I wasn't home; otherwise, they curled up with me on the mattress. Comfortable and safe, their fur had turned pink rather than camouflaged. Their white-striped, long, and fluffy tail clung on the shower rod and loosened as they climbed down the curtain upside down. The bathroom smelled of their cinnamon scent. I reached out my arms and they launched for my chest with a happy whistle. Their long, loose ears flopped, and short translucent wings sprang out and flapped once. They landed with no more weight than a large cat and without the sharp claws. Huge eyes gazed into mine as they held onto the straps of my tank top and braced hind feet on my belly; their wings folded and disappeared under a fluff of bright pink fur.

"Hungry?" I scratched under their ears exposing the tan fur below, and they whistled in contentment. "Noodles?" I asked turning for the kitchen.

We both liked noodles. I walked across the empty living room floor and circled the gray speckled counter. Inside a dented white fridge, I found the bowl of ramen left from lunch. Woo jumped to the counter in anticipation and sat on their haunches with tail curled like one of the bouncy squirrels in the back lot. Delicate hands reached for the piece of noodle I offered. My stomach growled before I sucked in a savory wad myself.

"I've got to shower." I broke off a number of noodles and laid them over the edge of the bowl, grabbing a second portion of salty ramen for my own appetite.

Woo whistled an acceptance with a slightly mournful note. They liked it when we ate together.

After my shower I slurped up the last of the ramen, rinsed the bowl, and headed for bed. Woo launched to the mattress with a single flap of wings began to clean their tail in a cat-like manner with a tiny pink tongue. Chilled, I pulled covers over my bare shoulders and checked my phone. Tyler hadn't texted, and I considered telling them about my excursion with the wildling. Woo climbed up my arm to stare at my phone from my shoulder. Tyler was still a little uncomfortable about discussing Woo or people they called cryptids.

I whispered into Woo's ear. "I can talk with Vivianne in the morning." Previous messages from Tyler waited on my screen, but I hadn't typed anything.

Woo whistled, as if agreeing. I couldn't be sure how much they understood.

Sighing, I put my phone down and tussled the short fur on Woo's head and stroked down their ears. "Let's get some sleep."

I wasn't sure they could actually fly because the thin translucent wings were so small, but they almost always flashed when Woo jumped down.

I wrapped the warm blankets around me and curled so Woo could nestle under my chin. Tomorrow morning I'd grab some tea for my friend Vivianne and let her know about my jaunt with the wildling. I should have remembered his name. She'd be delightfully mortified of course, but it seemed all Fae had an aversion to wildlings.

CHAPTER 2

THE NEXT MORNING I left the Square Mug Café with two fragrant hot teas and a pastry in a bag. Vivianne hadn't been hungry, but always welcomed tea. Traffic rumbled on Famu Way behind the buildings of the Railroad Square Art District, and a baby cried from the same direction near the vintage store. I strolled a presently quiet street that led to Vivianne's workplace. There were no tourists this time of the morning.

I texted Tyler. "WHAT ARE YOU UP TO?" I could never know if it was too early for them.

"ZAN AND I ARE ORGANIZING AN IMMIGRATION PROTEST. THEY'RE GOING TO MAKE IT SO ONLY THE WEALTHY HAVE A CHANCE TO IMMIGRATE."

Immigrate? I thought to Khimmer.

Moving from one country to another, Mistress.

Why would anyone care about that? I rarely understood Tyler's causes, but I was sure I'd hear more when I visited later in the day. I found the image of the smiling round head I used when I didn't know what else to reply. Tyler replied with another.

A gray car passed me, heading in the same direction. It turned across from Fat Cat Books and parked on tan grass beside the warehouse that held the craft house. All the buildings in the community were massive steel sheds built during a time when a nearby railroad had been important. I found the impossible trains amazing, but they were archaic to Earth people such as Tyler.

Smaller buildings to my left were painted lovely purples, blues, and light blue-greens. They attached to each other in a row leading to Fat Cats Books. Vivianne's workplace had an awning over a porch with chairs set out for people to sit. A cool breeze fluttered ferns at the edge.

I set our drinks on the table on the porch and texted Vivianne, "I'M HERE." The bookstore and cat shelter wouldn't open for another couple hours, but they didn't mind if I came in to visit Vivianne.

I waited as the inner door opened and Vivianne skittered out to unlatch the screen door. She smiled, and her short blonde hair bobbed at her neck. My truthsense let me see beyond her glamor that hid her true features: overly large brown eyes and tall Fae ears that bristled with tufts of dark fur higher than her hair.

"You're up and about early," she said.

I handed her a tea. "I could have used more sleep." I grinned, but she didn't catch it.

"I've still got some stock left to put away. We had another donation." She shooed a lanky black cat from coming out the main door as we stepped inside. An air-conditioner rattled warm air into the room.

"I'll help."

Vivianne snorted. "Not much. You're lousy figuring out genre."

"I can sort by last name." I closed the door with my elbow and earned a meowling complaint from the black cat.

Vivianne worked through a cardboard box while I took books as she named the section where each belonged. Bookstores were weird that way, and Vivianne's shop didn't have that many shelves. Tyler's room had nearly a third of the books in the entire store, just not the same titles. I'd read most of the ones at their house.

When we finished the box, she arranged a few more crafted items that people donated before we settled into the chairs and the cats came for loving.

None of her coworkers were within earshot, but I searched the room dramatically, grinned, and whispered, "I had sex with a wildling."

Vivianne blinked and the top of her ears twitched. She swore. "Nails! What?"

"Actually, really good." I reached behind and touched the scratch on my back. "The claws get in the way."

"Are you crazy? You have to be." Vivianne's lips pursed. Her olive skin blushed as she whispered, "But good?" She laughed out loud at my exaggerated nods.

Vivianne let the lanky black cat jump to her lap. "Want to bring him on a double date? I'm assuming it's a him."

"It was, this time, and no." I had no feelings for the wildling, and still couldn't remember his name. I could probably find him at the bar I'd been going to, but I had no intention of getting involved. "You're still with Chip?"

Vivianne mocked being insulted. "It's only been a couple weeks. Yes."

The calico purred as I scratched under her chin. "I should meet this Fae; he must be quite the character if he hasn't run screaming for his life yet."

She tried not to smile as she huffed, but Vivianne

couldn't help but chuckle. "Chip wants to head down to the beach now that it's warming up. He said we should bring friends. You want to come, maybe with Tyler?"

I flushed at the comment. "Tyler's just a friend, but maybe." In truth, there was no one I'd rather go with. "But it's not a double date."

Vivianne touched her necklace. "Of course not."

I could sense she wasn't lying but didn't trust her tone.

Her phone dinged in her pocket, and she pulled it out, turned off an alarm, and headed for the front door. "Agh," she murmured.

I heard her unlatch the door. "Welcome to Fat Cats, have you been here before?"

I sighed, knowing the store would be busy soon. Laura, my Nedjir friend, wouldn't be at her art studio for another hour or so. Tyler might be up for skating or have something fun we could do. I didn't expect my boss Bill to call with work on a Saturday. I rose, annoying the calico.

I'd call Tyler on the way to my apartment, and if they didn't want to do anything, I'd come back and tell Laura about the wildling. It would be different than the conversation with Vivianne; Laura was married, and the Nedjir were related to the wildlings. I smiled. Still, it would be fun to see her expression. She would somberly tell me all the dangers of such a liaison, but she always did that.

I waved goodbye to Vivianne as I opened the front door to leave.

CHAPTER 3

THE SCREEN DOOR clattered behind me, and the air had warmed somewhat with the Earth's sun rising in the sky. I still hadn't gotten used to its apparent movement. Emergency sirens whined from deeper in the city near College Town, Bill's office, and the Ramnath family house where Tyler lived with their sister Deanna and her gruff boyfriend John.

Railroad Square held more people as the day progressed, tourists ogling the painted walls and peering into shops and studios. A dark-haired man in a business suit strolled down the side of the dusty road toward me. At a bench on a gray-green lawn, two men ate with an unhurried pace. Cars had filled most spaces, and soon others would circle looking for available parking. Sometimes I was grateful I didn't drive, but I only lived a few minutes away on the other side of the tracks.

I dug for my phone as I walked, my back warmed by the rising sun.

A dark-haired man approached me, adjusting to intercept my path home. "Ahnjii Fate?" He strode with an assured gait that fit his solid form and above average height, as if a confident general or royal councilor.

I slowed and nodded. He could have been a lawyer. Bill dressed like that for court, but some of the other tenants of the office building wore suits, and they weren't lawyers. Despite the man's affable expression, I sensed an arrogant hunger in him — and more that I couldn't identify. "Hello."

"Gregor Gehrke." He offered his hand in a Tallahassee greeting, and I shook it. His face was clean-shaven, and his features were smooth enough to make me guess his age at mid-thirties.

The oddness I sensed made me uncomfortable. We stood in the open at the side of the road that led to Famu Way. "What do you want?" I asked.

"Right to the point, I like that. I'm a businessman myself and appreciate a clear negotiation." His eyes flicked toward the closest businesses. "You are a witch, a rather strong one from what I'm told, so I assume you know that I am an Upre."

I focused on the broad lapel that covered his left chest. Laura had said that the symbiont wrapped around the human host's heart. *What do you see, Khimmer?*

There is a warmer creature inside this human, Mistress. Besides the mass in the chest, it has tendrils leading to most vital organs and nerve clusters.

I shivered. Since dealing with Shailagh, a high Fae, and other non-human people on Earth, I'd started to let them assume I knew what being a witch meant and hid my ignorance as best as I could. I didn't want them to figure out I was from Duruce where the only people were humans. "And?" I asked him.

"I wish to offer you a standard contract for the sum of ten million dollars." He paused as if I should have reacted.

"That is a generous payment, I must admit. But you do offer unique abilities."

Chills spread down my neck into my shoulders.

Standard contract, Khimmer?

Contract is a binding agreement, Mistress. Standard, in this case, would require a reference or more context for a supposition.

"Standard?" I asked before regretting the question. It would highlight my ignorance, and I had no desire to be in a binding agreement with Gregor the symbiont-human Upre under any circumstances. "No, thank you."

Gregor stiffened and frowned. "If you have specific clauses, I'm sure I can make accommodations if they are outside the crucial components: our host's death, compelling, and the integration."

I had a lot of questions for Laura. Of all my non-human friends, she seemed the least suspicious of my ignorance. "No, thank you." Did witches actually agree to this?

Anger flashed over Gregor's features. "Twelve million."

I shook my head and uncomfortably glanced down the road. I'd have to walk around him. I'd never considered the Upre before. How *did* they get human hosts?

"Twenty million."

I imagined that would be an attractive amount for most humans on Earth. Their sense of economics was beyond me, but it would pay for a lot. Even on Duruce many were swayed by money. I couldn't imagine making such a gruesome agreement. I locked my jaw to avoid grimacing. Gregor had a human host, so someone had agreed.

"I need to go home. Thank you for the offer," I said politely.

Rage tinged Gregor's tone. "You live in a ghetto. Twenty million would change that."

Ghetto? I thought to Khimmer.

A poor and undesirable neighborhood, in this context, Mistress.

I turned with a nonchalant shrug. "I like my apartment."

"You have nothing. You don't even own a car."

"Don't drive one. Don't need one."

"You would live like a queen before and after integration; you would want for nothing."

Integration?

A supposition only, Mistress, the introduction of the symbiont into a human host.

I finally grimaced and suppressed a shudder as I imagined something crawling around inside of me. Gregor gave me the creeps. "I don't think it's a good fit for me." I snickered at my own dark humor. Tyler would have appreciated it.

Gregor's upper lip raised, showing neat, white teeth and his face twisted into a snarl around his wrinkling nose. "You have no idea what you're risking if you make an enemy of me."

"It sounds like any deal with you is a risk. I'll pass."

He reached out quickly to grab my arm, but I easily dodged him. "I can make your life miserable," he growled.

"I gathered that from your original offer." I stepped back, sensing his desperation. His demeanor had shifted so quickly I gathered that he'd expected me to quickly agree to his offer. Some people don't handle rejection well.

Gregor's expression turned to full rage, and he lunged to attack me. He favored his right, so I shifted to his left and easily blocked his wrist.

I used a little more force than was necessary. As his arm

flew toward his chest, Gregor stumbled off balance and fell to one knee. He jumped to his feet in a flurry of dust.

I stood ready, feet squared to my shoulders and hands loose at my sides. "You've gotten your nice suit dirty and have caused quite the scene." I tilted my head without taking my eyes off him.

Across the road in the parking lot, a couple stood at the open door of their SUV with a paper bag in hand. They were watching us. Neither had reached for their phones. The two men eating lunch at the picnic table chanced quick peeks over their shoulders.

Gregor straightened, leaned down to brush off his knee, and relaxed his expression to a deadly cold glare. "This isn't over." He turned with a sharp step and briskly strode away.

I remained still, steadily breathing in and out. The altercation had my blood pumping. Heading home would mean following in the same direction as Gregor Gehrke, and I wanted to be nowhere near him. What did he know about me? I had to learn more about the Upre, and quickly. They seemed more dangerous than the high Fae and wildlings combined and certainly quick to anger.

My pulse pounded in my ears, distorting the sounds of nearby traffic. The exhaust mixed with a sweet barbeque that trailed in the breeze. Laura would answer my questions about the Upre. I'd grab lunch at the Crum Box, then head to her studio. She had said she would be in around lunchtime, and I intended to meet her when she arrived.

CHAPTER 4

Laura dropped her brush. It clattered and splattered red paint on the toes of Nightarmor's boots and across the already colorful concrete. "You can't do it." Her tiny, feline-shaped mouth formed a pink circle. The hair stood on the gently curved ears atop her round head, making her face look even more catlike than usual. She sat in front of her easel that held the light sketch of a new painting. Her finished work dotted the cavernous space.

Still rattled from Gregor despite a long lunch, I leaned down to pick up her brush. "I didn't accept, of course. Sorry. I should have started with that."

"How did an Upre learn about your truthsense? My family has been very careful with your secret, ever since Shailagh found out."

Laura didn't know about Nightarmor, only Tyler, Shailagh, and a group of wildlings in Orlando who had witnessed it changing. I doubted Gregor knew. "Do you think he wants my truthsense? Does it work like that?"

Huge red eyes wide, Laura bobbed her head. "Yes, yes. That's why they often contract empaths — witches. You never know how it might work out with a death's contract. An Upre usually has three or four agreements at one time. When their host dies, they'll pick from the best option, though you would be the top choice of any. So, a witch might die naturally and never have to become host. It's like the human lottery for witches. Many take it, if the payment is high enough, and it always is substantial."

I frowned and shook my head. "I can't imagine choosing that."

"Neither could I, and there are some witches who don't accept. The Upre understand."

My eyebrows raised. "Not this Gregor Gehrke. He had a livid fit. Threatened me that I'd regret it and that it wasn't over."

Laura studied me, scratching her fur high on her head, just under the ear. "That's unusual for an Upre. They are inordinately consumed with power, but as impeccable about their presentation and appearance in all things. In business they will smile to your face while ruthlessly cutting your legs out from under you, metaphorically speaking. You should be careful when dealing with them." She pursed tiny lips. "I wonder why he would act so?" Her human finger contrasted her face as she touched her lip. "You should be wary."

I would have Tyler, whose skills on Earth's internet were the best I could imagine, research this Gregor Gehrke. "What can you tell me of the Upre?"

Her tiny nostrils flared. "They are disliked by the Fae and Nedjir, and always have been from the poems. The symbiont survives by drinking blood, like a mosquito. Humans used to call them vampires. They have to make contracts, different than what you're being offered, to drink human blood; they mainly feed on bovine."

I leaned forward. "What?"

"The blood contracts started long before any history we have, as did the death contracts. Something to do with the wars back then. The Upre, the high Fae, and even the Nedjir were —are — bound by those agreements. The Knights still impose those rules, and the high Fae Council, Upre, and ourselves abide by those accords." Laura waved her brush in dismissal. "Even wildlings are despised less than the Upre. Anyway, the Upre cluster in families related to their symbiont ties rather than their human hosts. The most powerful people in the world are Upre, owning mega corporations or ruling over countries." She paused and peered at me. "Why are you grinning like that?"

"Speaking of wildlings," I started.

An hour later, after we'd gotten past Laura's lecture on dallying with wildlings and she'd healed my scratch, I stepped out of her studio with the sun in its strange position directly overhead. The temperature had warmed nicely, though it still was not as hot as the Tallahassee summer had been. Months ago, it felt like I lived on the coast of Vale Aganor with a blistering sunside breeze.

I had not forgotten about Gregor and his threats, so I diligently peered at the tourists milling about. One stood out and brought a smile to my face. She had a good length of bright red hair and Fae ears that poked through curly locks. Shailagh walked down the opposite side of the street and checked traffic before angling toward me.

I bounced before jogging off to meet her. "Shailagh!"

A playful smile crept into her expression, and her gaze traveled down my hips and legs. She wore a simple blue blouse complimenting her various pieces of colorful jewelry and a thick green skirt below her knees. Waiting until I'd skipped to a stop in front of her, she replied, "Ahnjii. You look well."

The last time we'd seen each other had been when she'd helped rescue John and I'd killed the wight she wanted to keep alive. I hadn't been sure if she were still my friend. "You look great," I said. Grabbing my braid, I kept from hugging her. Shailagh didn't seem like the casual contact type, though she did want to bed me. Maybe she wasn't here for me at all. "How'd you find me?"

"You have a predictable pattern, for the most part." She offered me a sly grin, then her expression turned somber. "We need to talk about a couple things. Has Idin come around to question you?"

"Idin?"

Shailagh motioned me to a quieter section along the street where trees lined a fence beside the railroad tracks. "I was sure he would have by now. The Council is furious about Theovole, especially so soon after the rogue wildling debacle. Which is the other reason I'm here." Her expression had grown serious, and her tone had begun to take on the arrogance of the high Fae. She waited for me to respond.

"Idin, who's that?"

She positioned herself against a tree with furtive glances at the Railroad Square street and tourists. "An investigator, like myself, who handles the more serious situations. He's a brute, in my opinion. Idin has little care about humans, or any people other than high Fae, for that matter. He'll be contacting you about the incident with the wight's death. Be honest about Theovole's activities and death." Her lips tightened and she gestured along her own bare arms to indicate Nightarmor's bangles and armbands. "Except, you know. I told them you brought an iron spike of some sort."

Shailagh had agreed to keep her knowledge of Nightarmor from her high Fae Council, even after threatening that she should mention it. She seemed to believe they would cause me harm over it.

"Why should I even talk to him then? He doesn't sound like someone I'd like." I frowned. I should get Shailagh's input on Gregor while we were on the topic of nasty men.

"For my benefit, at the least. They were quite insistent that I should have handled your behavior better. They know about your *verity*." Shailagh cocked her head with a barely perceptible shrug, as if in apology. "That was unavoidable, considering you were not enthralled. A witch without your strength would have been easily controlled by a high Fae or wight, though none have tried for centuries."

She called my truthsense 'verity,' and I assumed it was a high Fae term. Her assumption that I was a witch I'd let drop and even tried to hide my ignorance. I didn't need anyone but Tyler believing I was from another world. Deanna knew, but I guessed that she thought it a lie to keep my past life hidden.

I nodded to let Shailagh know that I didn't blame her. "Okay, I'll be nice to this Idin. I wanted to ask you about the Upre."

"I've got other matters to discuss, if this can wait."

"It can, I guess." I shrugged, but pouted slightly. "I told him no anyway."

"Told who no? The Upre?"

Evidently, she was willing to discuss Gregor. "Yes, Gregor."

"He offered you a death contract?"

I resigned myself to standing at the side of the road. "Yes. Got really mad when I said no. Kept adding millions to the number, but I knew something was weird. I don't think I like Upre."

"What's your definition of really mad?" Shailagh raised a hand before I could respond. "I don't mean to be rude, but you are a little people-pleasing."

I pouted. Deanna and even Tyler had said the same. I didn't see it as a bad thing. "Well, he threatened that I was risking making an enemy of him, and it sounded like he thought I'd regret it. He tried to attack me, but there were witnesses."

Shailagh's eyebrows raised. "They are usually much more conservative than that." She thought for a moment. "You can be irreverent though. Did you make any of your snarky remarks?"

I shuffled and tried to remember my exact words.

"Of course you did. Still, it seems a little out of character for an Upre, though they are very used to getting what they want. How much did he offer? A million or two?"

"Twenty."

Her eyebrows, having worked their way down, bounced back up. "I've never heard that price for a contract. He must want your verity. It would be useful in business situations. Still." Shailagh looked down, absorbed her thoughts. "I don't imagine it will come to anything."

"He didn't seem done."

"What did he say?"

Exact words?

He said, "This isn't over," Mistress.

"This isn't over." I waited for her response, then explained, "He might have been pissed about his pants."

"Pants?"

"I told you he attacked me. I knocked him to the street."

"An Upre? They're faster and stronger than humans."

She drew a breath. "Though I have seen you fight. Be careful. You don't want an Upre for an enemy. That brings up the reason I'm here. Clarita is making noise in her pack that she needs to exact revenge on the both of us."

"We found the rogue for her." I'd been warned, and hadn't intended the wildling to jump on Nightarmor's spike. "It died by accident, and they were going to kill it anyway." Her warning had been clear, and I'd done the best I could to not kill the rogue wildling. However, he'd attacked me.

Shailagh shook her head. "I warned you. They don't take killing one of their own lightly, no matter the circumstance. Besides, she's having trouble holding her position as their leader and is looking for something to give them a focus." She waved long fingers between me and her. "Us."

"What will they do?" With Nightarmor, I didn't particularly fear the wildlings, but I tensed at the thought of them coming near the apartment and threatening Woo. They were all the way in Orlando, and they didn't have the benefit of Shailagh's tree portals.

"If Clarita gets them to move on us, they'll probably come looking for you, as that would be easier. I'd avoid any wildlings if I were you."

I bit my lip with a lopsided grin. "Oops."

"What did you do?"

"I've been sort of hanging out at a wildling bar the past couple of nights."

Shailagh threw her hands out to her sides in exasperation. "Why?"

"I was curious about sex with them when they were all . . ." I raised my shoulders to show bulk, but I doubted it had the effect I wanted. "I got it out of my system, mostly."

"Too late, but don't do that." She took a long breath,

studying me, then tapped her ear. "Keep in contact with me. Let me know the minute you see anything unusual. How good are you at sensing them?"

I'd left the earring she'd given me for us to stay in contact pinned through the sheet that covered the window in my bedroom. I had been able to use what she considered empath witch powers to a limited extent. "Better. Hanging at the bar gave me a better feel for it."

"You had sex at their apartment, not yours?"

I nodded.

"Good. I can only hope they don't remember you."

I hoped he'd not forget any time soon. "So, just keep my eye out?"

"Unless I hear something more solid from my contacts. I may have to approach Clarita directly with Council sanctions at that point."

Did she have a wildling contact in Clarita's clan? I wasn't sure if I could pick out a wildling in human form on the street, but I'd try. I wasn't about to allow them to hurt Woo.

My phone rang in my pocket, and considering the present tension in our conversation, I jumped. Shailagh waited with pursed lips as I interrupted our discussion to dig in my shorts.

Doris had called. I hadn't expected any work on a Saturday. "Work." I lifted the phone to indicate the importance before answering.

"Ms. Fate? Can you come in?" Bill's secretary had a pleasant voice.

I sighed. "Yes. When do you need me? Wait, proper shoes?"

The older woman chuckled on the other end of the phone. "Not today."

CHAPTER 5

I LEFT Shailagh after she finished with a few more warnings and admonishments, mainly not to have sex with or kill any more wildlings. Was Shailagh jealous?

I jumped the fence where no one in Railroad Square could see. Traffic and music sounded from College Town as I danced over the railroad tracks. The day had warmed, and the scent of steel and rock lingered before I jumped the next fence.

Doris had sounded like she was in the office from the rustling paper in the background of the call. Bill had a witness who could only come in this afternoon for a deposition. I cut through the parking lot by Publix and ignored the option to get some boba tea. It would be available on the way back home.

I walked toward two hefty-sized men coming the opposite direction on the same street, and found my pulse quicken. In their thirties, they were too old to be students.

I tried to sense them and see if they were wildlings. One had a tightly trimmed full beard and did seem to be watching me. They did seem off to me, but I was feeling a little paranoid.

Any wildlings nearby? I thought to Khimmer.

None that I detect, Mistress. In human form, their temperature is only elevated by a minuscule amount.

I blushed, feeling foolish. We were only a few steps away from passing on the sidewalk when I began to wonder about Gregor's threats. My pulse beat in my ears.

The one without the beard I could tell smiled. He nodded. "Hey."

I kept a fluid step, ready for a skirmish. My voice squeaked slightly. "Hey."

They passed and I listened to their footsteps.

I'm being foolish.

Practical and observant, Mistress. Turben always taught you to take every situation with care.

My ears warmed at my mentor's name. *I'm not an assassin here on Earth. I don't have to expect a blade from every corner.* The air smelled of pizza, and my stomach growled.

Perhaps, Mistress.

I would not let Clarita and Gregor turn my life on Earth into an exercise from the Aegis monks.

Don't mention Turben's name.

Yes, Mistress.

It still turned out to be an uncomfortable walk to Bill's office building. The buildings grew taller, and more people crowded the sidewalks. The air stunk of exhaust.

I rode the elevator up to Bill's office and glared at my reflection in the polished doors. I wouldn't live constantly waiting for the next attack.

Doris was typing at her computer as I came around the corner. She was dressed in her usual office attire as if this were any other workday. Bill had said they rarely worked Saturdays. That did not mean never.

She flicked a glance at me from under her light hair, gestured toward clothes hanging over the chair in front of her desk, and went back to typing. "Not court, but I still think you should wear those."

It looked like a blue-green blouse and dark slacks. I touched the straps of my bodysuit as I approached. "I didn't think I needed to dress up." I had purchased long pants and a long-sleeve shirt. They were the only clothing hanging in my bedroom closet.

Doris shrugged. "It'll only take a minute." She seemed to type one handed as she pointed to the bathroom around the corner. "They're all here. Waiting on you."

I swallowed and grabbed the clothes. Ten minutes later I had most of Nightarmor's jewelry hidden, their boots covered, and Doris had my shorts.

"Ms. Fate, sorry for the last minute call. I'm glad you were available." Bill tapped the pad of paper laying upside down on the seat beside him. He wore a dark blue suit that wrinkled and didn't seem to fit his somewhat pudgy body well.

Across from him sat a young woman in black who looked like she'd swallowed something sour.

The woman who caught my eye sat at the far end dressed in pale purple, with a ready smile and a collection of equipment in front of her. She had brown hair loosely tied back and dark eyes that studied all of us. Bill rarely brought a scribe in to take notes on their Earth machines, and never one so beautiful. I paused before sitting to give her a hearty grin.

We all had to give our full names. Bill stated some details about the case and the frowning woman sitting across from us, but that was none of my concern. I glanced at the nearly full page of writing on the yellow pad. As usual, Doris had written a list of questions Bill wanted me to truthsense. When I sat back, Bill's bulbous nose blocked the cute girl taking notes on her machine.

Bill had a casual, friendly tone, almost always. "Let's start with your location when you witnessed my client. You were walking west along the north side of East Jefferson Street approaching the crosswalk over South Adams Street?"

The black-haired woman's face pinched tighter. "Yes."

Lie. The sense of lying washed over me as if I had spoken it. Writing pad leaning from my lap to the table, I sketched an awkward F next to the first question. Bill casually noted my answer. Why would this woman lie about where she was? I wouldn't understand his question from all the easts and wests, but people from Tallahassee did.

"It was from this position you stopped, turned around, and witnessed my client, Levi Williams, leaving the American Institute of Architects?"

"Yes."

Lie. I marked another fat F next to the second question. From the lineup of questions, Bill always had a good sense about what someone would lie about. Sometimes he tackled them at the beginning, and others at the end.

"You were not across the street in front of the City Hall?"

The woman snorted. "No, I was not."

Lie. She lied well, sounding affronted, but my truthsense didn't rely on tone or expression. I felt it.

The rest of the questions appeared innocuous, and she only lied about where she was heading. I'd grown used to Bill enough to know that he already had a plan in place to break down her testimony. A witness lying on record often gave him some leverage. I peeked past his face to the woman taking notes. She smiled. I'd hang a little while and try and get her number, or even see if she wanted to spend some time together this afternoon. Someone wore a light, flowery perfume.

I sat back and took a deep breath. Between Clarita and Gregor, I should be careful. Perhaps I would go hang with Tyler. The Upre mystified me. Wildlings I understood.

When we finished with the liar and she'd quickly strode out of the room, I hoped to get a chance to talk with the scribe, but Bill led me out to Doris. "Monday I'm going to need to find cameras of the courthouse. Order these pages." He jerked a thumb back toward the room where the brown-haired woman packed up her machines. He patted my shoulder. "Thanks for coming out on short notice. Nice shirt."

As Doris handed me my shorts, folded into a neat pile, I felt puffy in the clothes, like I was playing a noble. I hadn't had to make any notes, and she could tell my Fs from Ts. She was standing when I came out of the bathroom. The scribe had left.

I needed to find out what I could about the Upre and had already talked to Laura and Shailagh. Tyler might be able to look up Gregor's name, and Vivianne might have a different view of them than a high Fae like Shailagh did. I'd head back to Fat Cats and see what I could get from her before heading to Tyler and Deanna's house.

I handed Doris the clothes. "Thank you."

She nodded. "Picked them up at the thrift store, just to have here. I didn't think the ASA would show up for this deposition on a Saturday, but better to be prepared. Have a good night."

I headed for the door and the elevators beyond. *ASA? Unknown acronym, Mistress.*

I did not understand the difference between a deposition and an interview. They seemed the same. I didn't need to know most of the terms; I just told Bill when people lied.

I had bigger concerns about the Upre and what threat Gregor posed. On the way to talk to Vivianne, I would grab some boba tea.

CHAPTER 6

Dusty scents met me as I stepped inside the cat rescue and bookstore, and I closed the screen door with a clatter. Vivianne was talking about the different sections of books from deeper in the store. I knelt by the calico, slurping up sweet tapioca balls as I scratched her chin. Some nearby candles wafted vanilla and spice into the air.

I'd need to get home to feed Woo before heading to Tyler and Deanna's.

While Vivianne sold a couple books to a middle-aged woman who kept brushing fur from her slacks, I busied myself drinking my tea and moving from one cat to the next.

"Didn't expect to see you back," Vivianne said as the exiting customer banged the front door behind herself. "You started thinking about that beach trip, didn't you?" Her smile grew conspiratorially.

After checking the back for coworkers, I leaned on the counter. "What do you know of Upre?"

Her smile disappeared and the tufted tips of her tall ears twitched. "Why?"

I detailed my encounter with Gregor, waving off her

interruptions of "Don't" multiple times before we got to his aggressive behavior. He sounded even more desperate in my rendition.

"Nails, Ahnjii. What are you going to do?" Vivianne had become animated during my story, but leaned on the counter to speak in a hushed voice.

"That's what I wanted to ask you. What do you know of them? Are they prone to violence?" I wasn't going to mention the Clarita issue; I'd been chastised enough about my overnight involvement.

"They are dangerous, just not usually in a physical way. The Upre do well in human society. Politics and business. Those are the stories I hear. I've never heard of any of them outright attacking anyone. But, you are annoying."

I chuckled at the comment though mostly to hide my disappointment and concern. "Maybe that's it. So, nothing to worry about?"

She studied me. We'd only been friends a few months, and I'd never had friends before coming to Earth, but she and Tyler read my emotions well. "You're not that foolish. Too trusting at times, but this isn't one of them. He might be all bluster. You might have just pushed his buttons. Either way, be careful."

"I'm worried about Woo being home alone."

Vivianne had only visited us once, but she smiled. "Your camouflaging companion? If they're like cats I know, they'd never find them." A door slapped open from the back room, and she jerked straight.

It was close to the end of their day, and two of Vivianne's coworkers came into the store and began cleaning and straightening. I said quick goodbyes and headed outside.

The sun had finally moved toward the horizon into

what was closer to a comfortable position for me. Traffic had thickened along Famu Way, and the air felt cool as I walked toward my apartment. The breeze brought the scent of the lake and a bit of chill with it.

An orange moving van was parked out front, one of Mrs. Forster's flamingos had been knocked over, and the "For Rent" sign was gone. As I jogged for the stairs, I peered into the downstairs window of the apartment that had been available. If someone had moved in, I didn't see them. They were directly below my apartment.

I beat Mrs. Forster to the door, and Woo scolded me as I locked it. "I'm sorry. A lot going on today."

Tyler had confirmed that Woo was not any Earth creature. They hadn't come from Duruce, and that bothered me. I ran to the cabinets as Woo whistled and worked their way out to the kitchen.

"Cat treats?" I asked.

Their whistle was less than excited. Woo got most excited about pistachios, but Tyler thought I should work in some variety beyond those and noodles. As Woo climbed up, I sprinkled a handful on the counter and popped one in my mouth. Tuna something hadn't gotten any tastier since the last time I tried. I preferred pistachios as well.

"You know anything about Upre?"

Woo whistled, and their pale fleshy whiskers extended to grab one of the square brown treats and push it into their tiny lips. I heard crunching, but had never seen teeth.

"You need to be careful. I've pissed some people off lately. Someone shows up while I'm gone, you hide."

Woo managed to whistle while they ate.

I checked Woo's water bowl in the bathroom, peed, and gave them a hug. "I'm heading to Tyler's. I'll be back soon." They let out a quiet low whistle as I headed out the door.

I still didn't spot my new neighbor on the way out, and Mrs. Forster's door didn't crack open until I hit the street. She said something, but I strolled toward the student apartments without looking back. Tyler might be cooking dinner, not that I planned to show up for their food.

The paranoia I'd felt earlier had eased, and people getting into their cars no longer seemed suspicious. I would be careful, but Vivianne had been right that Woo's ability to camouflage would keep them safe.

Tyler and Deanna's mansion, which they called a house, rested on a small estate with a number of other affluent neighbors. There was also a bank across the street, smaller houses, and a daycare next door. I'd thought it a family with a lot of children for months.

Deanna's SUV was gone, but Tyler's car was parked in front of the garage. I came in the back gate by the warehouse-sized building that housed their basketball court. Tyler might be encouraged to roller skate, unless their internet protest was still going on. If that were the case, it would be a boring evening.

"Tyler?" I climbed the stairs up to the second floor. One of Deanna's tabbies answered.

I passed my old room and found Tyler packing a backpack. "You're leaving?"

Tyler wore their usual black long-sleeve shirt, jumped at my arrival, and pulled an earbud from under their black hair. "Hey. I should have sent you a text. Me and Zan are heading out for a protest tomorrow."

I tossed my braid over my shoulder and flicked the ends. "Where?" I'd only met the handsome Zan once, and Tyler said they were just friends, but the man had seemed to have other interests.

"Pensacola. There will be another here in Tallahassee

Thursday morning." Tyler slid their laptop case into the pack. They hadn't bothered with any eye makeup today, a sure indication they had been preoccupied. "Sorry I'm bailing on you tonight. What have you been up to today? I thought you'd come by earlier."

"Work." *Pissing off a blood-sucking Upre who wants my human body.* "Is twenty million a lot?"

Tyler frowned. "Is Bill suing for harassment of one of his clients? Yes, that would be a lot to win in a court case. People kill for that kind of money."

Gregor had been desperate if he offered that much more than what Shailagh thought normal. How far would he go? Vivianne and Laura hadn't seemed worried. Shailagh was more concerned with Clarita. Wildlings might attack me anywhere. I should have locked the gate.

I didn't listen as Tyler discussed their protest plans, and suddenly I was very happy they were getting out of Tallahassee.

"I think it's a great idea. But I'll miss you." I would, though I'd be happier to see Tyler away from Clarita or Gregor.

Tyler tilted their head in a nod that seemed a shrug. "You could come along."

I dropped onto his bed, leaned back, and stretched. "I've got less time with a job and taking care of Woo. Besides, I still plan on going dancing Friday." My grin widened when Tyler glanced at me. "It'll be fun, just not as much as when you're there."

"I'll be back Monday."

My chest felt lighter with one less concern. Maybe this would all blow over by then.

CHAPTER 7

By the time I walked home, the sun had dropped over the horizon, leaving the eerie darkness of Earth's night in the sky above. Clouds and haze left only the brightest stars to shine; I liked that part of the dark.

Music played from my new neighbor's apartment. A stark bulb shone in the front window, but still I saw no one. Mrs. Forster's flamingos had been straightened.

Woo whistled at my return, and I headed for the kitchen to fill the tea kettle. "Hot ramen?"

Tyler had been on their way out, so I'd left without dinner. I could have cooked myself something there; Deanna wouldn't have minded, but Woo needed something to eat too.

Woo ambled into the kitchen and climbed the wood cabinet to the countertop with an appreciative whistle. I peeked under the kettle to make sure the metal had started glowing hot. My stove still baffled me. Tyler and Deanna had gas burners, and those made sense. "Going to be a few minutes."

I opened a package of noodles and broke the block into

quarters in my bowl. Woo waited until I was finished before whistling for a hug. They climbed onto my chest and buried the top of their head under my neck.

"If somebody nasty comes in here while I'm gone, you're going to camouflage, aren't you?"

They let out a low whistle. Woo knew my friends' voices and hadn't turned from pink to camouflage past the first meeting or two. A loud knock at the door was usually enough to make them blend into wherever they were hiding.

With little else to do, I read one of Tyler's books after we ate. Woo curled against my stomach. I'd overreacted about Gregor, and it felt good to relax and cuddle on my mattress.

I woke to a low whistle in my ear. Woo had never made that sound before. Naked except for the choker, belt, and arm pieces, I kicked off the covers with a shiver.

"What is it Woo?" Hopefully the cat treats hadn't made them sick.

Scampering silently and faster than I'd ever seen, Woo raced to the living room. Their nails scratched against the kitchen cabinets as they climbed in the darkness. Their pink coloring was gone. I swallowed and stopped before I turned on the kitchen light.

They let out the same low whistle as they peeked over the edge of the window, and I lost sight of them.

Earth's night left nothing to see when I first came to the window. The cars in the back parking area took on shape and color as I stared. The oak trees beyond were dark green canopies over pitch black.

Something moved in the inky depths under the trees.

Khimmer, is something out there?

Yes, Mistress.

Upre?

No, Mistress. I am sure it is a male wildling.

My pulse began to rise. I searched where I'd seen the motion, but could make out no detail. They were watching my apartment.

I considered calling for armor.

They are moving away, Mistress.

Had they spotted us? A prickling of my scalp crawled to a chill down my neck. I might have to take Shailagh's warning more seriously. *Don't overreact.*

Helmet.

Yes, Mistress.

Nightarmor poured over my head, replacing my vision with Khimmer's. A dark orange shape crept through the woods toward the water.

I could go after them, but if they attacked, I might accidentally hurt them. I assumed this was one of Clarita's pack. If Shailagh hadn't warned me, I'd likely think it was last night's sexual encounter back for another round; he didn't know where I lived, though.

Woo appeared a dull orange at the corner of the window. I crouched lower to expose only as much of myself as needed to watch the retreating figure. I thought of the high Fae earring jabbed into the sheet by my bed.

"Thank you, Woo."

The orange glow of the wildling faded, leaving the night monotone in Khimmer's vision. Would they come back? Perhaps bring the whole pack?

Any more, Khimmer?

No, Mistress.

The bowl in the sink still smelled of ramen, despite the water soaking in it. Woo hadn't moved. Could they still see the wildling?

We stood there for what seemed like forever before I finally backed away and slid to the floor.

Remove helmet.

Nightarmor poured off my face. Woo stayed vigilant. I'd have to contact Shailagh and let her know. More than ever, I was glad that I'd moved out of Deanna and Tyler's house, and that Tyler had left for their protest, even if they'd gone with Zan.

Gregor appeared to be less of a threat than Clarita. I wanted to face her and get it over with. I'd rather deal with the consequences than sit on my kitchen floor waiting for someone to smash through a window.

I'd have to do something about this, but I wasn't leaving Woo alone to go chase the wildling.

I DIDN'T SLEEP WELL, though Woo and Khimmer seemed satisfied that our stalker had moved on. After I hit the bathroom, I stumbled into the kitchen where the sky was the strange gray that came before the sun rose. I didn't turn on the light when I boiled water in the tea kettle. The woods out back were dark, but I could see into them.

Last night I had pulled out Shailagh's earring and had Khimmer affix it to my lobe with an ornate clip, but I hadn't reached out to her. *Visitor-Skulking-Wildling,* I sent through the sigils. I didn't want to give her the images since she did not know about that part of Nightarmor or Khimmer. *Last night.*

I stared out the window as I waited for her response, and started when the kettle whistled. Woo mimicked the sound from the counter where they ate leftover ramen. I poured hot water over the waiting tea strainer and pulled the chain up and down absently.

I sensed her concern when she responded; her impressions, emotions, and words blended. *Wildling? Sure?*

Shailagh assumed that most of my confidence came

from being a capable empath witch, but I had never even tried sensing people's emotions before she mentioned it. Until I'd come to Earth, I'd never heard the title. I let her continue in the belief rather than guess that I wasn't from here.

Yes.

Visit today - maybe.

I took a sip of hot tea that had a nutty tone to it and stared at the parking lot and woods. Clarita's pack would be an issue, and I had to wonder how they found my apartment. Probably followed me home after one of my visits to the wildling bar.

I couldn't sit around the house all day and peer out the kitchen window, so after a cup of tea, I threw on a clean, black tank top, yanked my phone off the charger, and snuck out the front door hoping that Mrs. Forster wouldn't hear.

The new neighbor had a short mop of sandy hair, a lanky form, and jeans cut short at the ankle. Otherwise, the pants fit fine. His left foot held open his torn screen door. He propped a plastic crate against the door while he rummaged for his keys. The rusting gray lamp above him had no bulb and just enough plant debris to give the hint at an abandoned bird's nest.

Key in the lock, he turned at my footfalls on the steps. "Hey." He had a pleasant smile and an easy voice with an accent that reminded me of a Tahnet merchant.

"Hey." I pointed up the stairs. "Ahnjii. Right above you."

He opened his door and settled the crate in both hands to turn. "Oliver Sweeney from Hartford, Connecticut. I moved down here to get out of the cold and am looking for work in food service." His words rattled out a bit too fast, as if nervous.

I chuckled. "Okay, Oliver. After you get settled I can show you around College Town, plenty of jobs there."

Oliver beamed. "That would be great."

Mrs. Forster slid one of the locks on her door. "Later." I danced through the flamingos and studied the street.

Khimmer. Any Upre or wildlings?

No, Mistress.

Keep an eye out.

Yes, Mistress.

Oliver seemed nice and a little awkward in a cute way. I'd avoid having sex with him since he'd be living so close.

I turned right on the street, wanting a quiet path. I'd go along Famu Way where both Khimmer and I would have a good view. If a wildling was going to follow me, I wanted to know about it.

CHAPTER 9

I spent the morning walking through the quiet Railroad Square as the sun rose, then into College Town, though nothing was open at this time of the morning. The street smelled of stale beer. Cars growled on the outer edges of the neighborhood where the large streets bordered. No matter where I went, neither Khimmer nor I found anyone suspicious following and certainly no wildlings.

No one? I thought to Khimmer as I headed back toward the Square Mug Café.

None, Mistress. Are you disappointed?

Perhaps. Confronting this head on would be preferable to waiting. I'd suggest to Shailagh that we go to Orlando again. She might not agree. I could have Tyler take me there, but I had trouble figuring out how to keep them from getting involved beyond that point. The wight had been a near disaster that I didn't want to repeat.

I found myself at the Square Mug and sat outside, sipping a light tea while I pondered my situation. No tourists would show up for a couple hours, and beyond the occasional tenant coming for the café, I had the chirping birds for company along with Khimmer. The air seemed almost fresh with only the slightest hint of the exhaust that hung in the city. I hadn't come up with a better plan.

When I spied Laura driving past in her dusty old car, I left my haunt at the café in a jog, hoping for some of Laura's somber judgment. I caught up with her as she unlocked the door, and we entered together.

"You look upset." Laura used a stick to turn on the switch. The Nedjir didn't do well near electricity. Bright lights high on the ceiling thudded and lit the warehouse studio.

"We had a wildling lurking outside the apartment last night. Woo spotted it and woke me."

Laura paused as she bent to lean the stick against the wall. "Your lover? I wouldn't have expected it, but wildlings are unpredictable."

"No, I don't think so." I had considered the idea, but assumed it more likely this had to do with Clarita. "Shailagh found me yesterday. It seems that Clarita, the new clan leader of that wildling pack in Orlando, is stirring up trouble and threatening to exact some revenge on Shailagh and me."

"And they know where you live?"

"I'm guessing so."

Laura's small lips tightened into a frown. "Then you need to move. Hide. You can't take on a whole pack. Killing any one of them will just reinforce their intention to kill you."

Outside of going home to complete my duty, I had no desire to give up my new friends and life. "Can't I just reason with them?" I slumped against the wall. Shailagh had been clear that this had been more politics than anything, and I didn't do well in that area.

Laura bobbed her head with a tilt. "Wildlings have certain needs that are usually supplied by high Fae, and even us Nedjir on occasion. Sigil work mainly to keep humans from wandering into their neighborhoods. They don't have the ability to bind the universal threads the way we do."

Shailagh would know their needs as well and have better opportunity to offer such services. That hadn't seemed an option in my discussion with her. I wasn't getting anywhere. "If it were that simple, Shailagh would have taken care of it already."

Laura's ears tilted forward in a droop. "You'll have to move," she said with a soft, sad tone.

My chest hollowed and a warmth flushed up my neck. I couldn't leave my friends and be alone again. "There has to be another way." If I hadn't been rooting around for sex with a wildling, Clarita might not even know where I lived. Shailagh had been clear and told me not to kill a wildling. I didn't have anyone to blame but myself.

Laura grabbed me in a hug. "I love you. I'm sorry."

I held her and my heart pounded in my ears. I spoke through gritted teeth. "I'm not leaving."

After a short one-sided argument with Laura while she let me vent, I stomped home from Railroad Square, angrier with every step I took. The wildlings had me trapped, but I'd made the mess. I could hope that Clarita was just bluffing. My visitor early this morning said otherwise. I needed to talk with Shailagh.

I slowed my gait and took a deep breath when Oliver opened his front door. The screen clattered as he let it close itself. He smiled when he spotted me, and I returned it with a reflexive attempt, though I couldn't push the anger away completely.

I swerved through the flamingos, and Oliver offered a handshake. His right hand had a pale scar just above his thumb, a straight line that pointed up his arm a hand's length. I'd seen similar on one of the Aegis monks from a sword fight, but Earth humans didn't use swords. Perhaps he'd had a kitchen accident.

His hand was warm, despite the cool air. "Didn't get much of a chance to say hello," he said.

"We didn't." I couldn't bring myself to want any company, but I didn't want him to think it was because of him.

Mrs. Forster exited her apartment with her broom, studying both of us. I wanted to be alone.

My phone rang in my pocket, and I sighed, grateful for the reprieve. I had told Oliver I'd show him around, but now was not the time.

Doris came up on the screen. Tyler had entered her contact information so I would know who called. I pointed to my phone. "Work."

He tugged at his collar and gestured as if for me to answer. "Understand." His accent really did remind me of home.

"Hi, Doris."

"Ahnjii, you'll want to come into the office right now."

Sunday. I frowned, watching Oliver fidget in a somewhat cute way. "Court?"

"No, can you pack for an overnight?" She cleared her throat. "It's Tyler, they've been arrested."

That made no sense. The skin on my arm tingled. "Why?"

"It's serious. Bill is acting as local council, though Deanna has Edward Miller, a family friend, coming in from the north. Deanna's flying to Pensacola as we speak. You and Bill will be following in a couple hours."

Tyler in jail? I felt a chill up my spine. The people there were miserable. "Pensacola?" My pulse started to race. My disaster of a day could not get any worse at this point.

"Yes, Pensacola. Can you be at the office in forty-five minutes?"

I nodded, but Doris couldn't see that. "Yes." My world seemed to speed up. "I'll be faster than that." Laura could check on Woo; I'd given her a key.

"Forty-five minutes is fine." Doris hung up.

I hung up, wide eyed. Jail was a horrible place, on Earth or home. They couldn't keep Tyler. The thought sickened me.

"Going to Pensacola?" Oliver asked.

I flew past him for the stairs. "Yes. Sorry."

I needed to pack. Usually I borrowed one of Deanna's bags. Taking two steps at a time, I heard Mrs. Forster's broom. I cleared the landing with a snarl. "Don't even start."

Mouth open, broom pressed motionless against polished concrete, she stared at me.

I growled as I shoved the key in the lock. What could Tyler have done? They'd protested before. I'd even helped carry signs with them. The police had been there and seemed bored at best. No one had been arrested.

The door unlocked and I flew inside as Mrs. Forster finally found her voice. "There's a reason you're always in a rush."

The room smelled of noodles and cinnamon. I ignored Mrs. Forster. *Khimmer, where is Pensacola?*

West of Tallahassee, Mistress.

It didn't help. With Earth's sun always moving, I had no sense of direction.

Left on the map, Mistress.

"If you'd take some time to look at your maladaptive tendencies . . ."

I slammed the door before Mrs. Forster finished.

Woo whistled excitedly from the bathroom, likely startled. Half camouflaged to the white and blue of the bathroom, they hung off the shower rod and grabbed hold of the curtain to climb down.

"Sorry." Residual anger over the wildlings and a growing panic over Tyler tightened my chest. I couldn't worry about Clarita at the moment. Deanna would be freaking. Bill might be able to use my truthsense to free Tyler, and that had to be my focus. It was the only way I could help.

I dialed Laura, pressed speaker, and threw the phone on the bed to begin packing. The only bag I had was from Publix and still had empty garbage from a sub and chips.

"Hi, Ahnjii." Her tone was sad.

"Laura. Can you come by and check on Woo? I've got a problem. I'm leaving. Tyler's been arrested."

"Yes. Of course. Why?"

I tossed out the trash with a whiff of vinegar and stuffed a pair of blue panties into the plastic bag. "Woo gets upset if no one visits. You know that."

"No. Why did they arrest Tyler?"

"Oh." I ran to the bathroom, leaping over Woo. "I don't know. I guess for protesting."

CHAPTER 10

WHEN I STEPPED out and locked my door, my phone chimed with a message. Mrs. Forster had gone back inside, but I still hurried, juggling my vinegar-scented bag while pulling out my phone. I didn't recognize the number.

"BEFORE THINGS GET WORSE FOR YOUR FRIEND, WE SHOULD CONTINUE OUR NEGOTIATION."

I stumbled on the steps, nearly falling. Oliver had left. The flamingos appeared bright in the morning light. Noises of traffic dulled to the blood pounding in my ears. I felt the heavy thud of my next step in my bones.

Had Gregor done this? Had he gotten Tyler arrested? The message had to be from him. What did he mean by worse? Another step echoed dully through my body. I'd caused this.

I couldn't battle this world of Gregor's with Nightarmor. My skills were insufficient. The woman who had betrayed me and caused me to kill my own parents, Gigina, could have handled his schemes. I had brought this all down on Tyler without any way to fix it. Phone in one hand and bag in the other, I stopped on the landing and stood there.

Turben and the Aegis monks had been right when they'd kept me from having friends. I hadn't been a danger to anyone there, and here I was a danger to Tyler and anyone else I cared about. *Damn me to Hades.* What was I supposed to do?

I could agree to Gregor's demands, insuring Tyler's release. My acceptance of the contract would mean nothing to me under these circumstances, but I still didn't understand them. Laura had mentioned the Knights enforcing something, which meant Darren McGyver, a witch, whom I didn't trust. She'd also mentioned the high Fae Council.

Bill and I might be able to free Tyler, and perhaps I would follow Laura's advice and leave. It might be the best for everyone.

I glared at the screen and closed it, hating to be out of control. There were few options, and I wasn't skilled enough to handle any of them, outside of ramming a sword through host and symbiont. Deanna and Bill would have a plan, and I should at least hear it first.

Mrs. Forster's voice broke into my world, and I leaped through her flamingos and broke into a run for Bill's office.

I had worked up a sweat by the time I reached Doris standing at her printer as it spit out pages. The room smelled acrid. She looked at the plastic bag in my hand and smiled. "I packed the clothes for you." The satchel she pulled from behind her desk had two large brown handles and a flowery design of every color. She unzipped it down the middle. "There's room for your bag inside. Bill wanted to make sure you had a carry-on and didn't intend to check anything. I didn't think it would be an issue."

I had no idea what not getting checked was, but nodded. "Thank you."

She motioned toward the chair in front of her desk. "Now the waiting begins. Coffee?" she asked.

I stuffed my bag inside the colorful satchel. "Okay." I didn't suppose they had tea. Dropping into the seat, I pulled up my braid and nervously flicked the ends with my left hand.

Doris hadn't been wrong about the waiting. I'd forgotten how long it took at airports with lines, the rooms full of chairs, and people climbing in and out of the strange airplanes. Khimmer had managed without Nightarmor during the security gate, and when the guards' wands still beeped at the back of my neck, I used the same story that worked when Deanna brought me to Venice. I told them I had a pin in my spine.

The worst was when I sat watching the airplanes driving across the massive parking lot, but we had to wait for a specific one. I'd been trained to wait, but this was personal and roiled my stomach. Bill bought me a book and more than one tea, but I couldn't stomach the idea of food.

"I'll be primary on this. Edward Miller is the big gun out of New York, a friend of the Ramnaths. He's good."

"That's good. Will we be bringing Tyler back with us?" I'd asked the question a number of different ways and each time Bill had been careful not to lie.

"Until we meet with the ASA, I can't determine how this is going to play out." He checked the time as he often did. "We've got a meeting scheduled at eight in the morning. That's when we'll get the details. They're being close-lipped about this. Edward already has motions ready for me to file."

My phone chimed, and a cold chill washed over me. I swallowed. "I'm going to use the bathroom."

The message, as I feared, was from Gregor. "Do NOT UNDERESTIMATE ME. REPLY."

The huge room hummed with a dull roar of noise. It stank of food, and I felt sick. People milled past, bored or in a hurry. They ate, focused on their phones, or laughed with family and friends. At the end of the row in front of me, a young girl sat at her parents' feet rolling a miniature car around three dragons. I would never be allowed to live like that.

I hated Gregor's world where Nightarmor and I couldn't protect the people I cared about. I'd been warned that friendships brought this fear — this risk.

My trust in Deanna and Bill jumped from hope to despair with every heartbeat, but I would wait until morning. If we couldn't free Tyler their way, then I'd agree to Gregor's demands. Laura had said that some people lived and died without ever having one of those creatures crawling around inside them. I shivered.

Somehow, I didn't believe Gregor intended me to get away with that.

I sucked in a breath and straightened. Bill hunched over his phone. I had to trust that his skills would help Tyler in the morning. If not, I would reply to Gregor.

CHAPTER 11

IN THE MORNING, I met Deanna in front of a strange building formed as if blocks had been stacked in a four-story pile. The cool, salt-tinged breeze carried the scent of the nearby ocean. Sirens wailed in the distance.

Deanna looked too thin, and her face hung gaunt. Dark shadowed under her eyes. "I'm glad you're here, Ahnjii." She gave me a hug, and her long black hair draped over my face.

I couldn't tell her this was my fault. She wouldn't believe the explanation. "Is Tyler okay?"

"They won't let me visit." Her tone hardened as if to steel. "Don't worry." Her haunted expression had turned to anger as she straightened. "Edward will get Tyler out." She looked Bill in the eyes. "He doesn't know the full extent of your ability. I just told him you were good at reading people."

Not good enough. I hadn't expected Gregor to attack my friends.

Across the street from us, a church had ornate steeples

as if to contrast the blocky building. Three birds circled a cross at the top. I could hear their laughing caws.

"Is that Edward Miller?" Bill asked.

I snapped around toward a tall man in dark suit. His red-striped tie flapped in the wind. His arrogance and build reminded me too much of Gregor, and I tensed.

Deanna breathed out a breath as if she'd been holding it all this time. "Yes." She strode to meet Edward and brought him back to us.

Calming his tie with his left hand, he carried a briefcase with his right. He studied us, never smiling even when he spoke. "William Buford. Ahnjii Fate."

Edward and Deanna led the way, and I followed with Bill who explained again that he would be the attorney of record, and I was to be his assistant. He leaned toward me so that only I could hear. "Tap your pad twice if the ASA or anyone with them lies. We'll ask them to repeat, or rephrase if there's any question about what they lied about."

I asked the question that had been haunting me through a near sleepless night. "Why would they lie?" I had no understanding of the accusations against Tyler, and Bill had been unsure as well. What had Gregor manipulated to put my friend at risk?

"Everybody lies," Bill said. "The key is, about what?"

The halls inside were cleaner than any I'd been in. The walls were as barren and plain as the outside. A young woman led us up an elevator and down a corridor, turning twice. I'd seen a couple jails, at home and with Bill, and this looked like none I'd ever seen.

My heart raced, hoping to find Tyler in this maze.

Can you see Tyler?

Khimmer took a moment before they responded. *I do not believe so, Mistress. There are some people who have similar dimensions, but they are not Tyler. There are people at the edges of my range that I have too little information to confirm or reject.*

Keep looking.

Yes, Mistress.

The young woman stopped and opened a door. The empty room could have been a larger version of where we talked to people at Bill's office. It smelled of plastic and cleaners, like right after Deanna's maids dusted her house.

The oval table had a silver tray in the middle with glasses and a pitcher of water. "I'll let Mr. Convery know that you are here." The young woman closed the door behind her.

Edward gestured for me to sit at the far end, then Bill slid in beside me. Edward settled in next, and Deanna took the seat closest to the door. It seemed odd to all sit on one side. That and the silence everyone held made my neck itch under the shirt Doris had packed for me. Bill and Edward both began laying folios on the table, and I received a blank yellow pad and a pen.

A door closed in the hallway, but no one came. Leaning on the table I could see Deanna and the door. I felt thirsty, with the water right in front of me, but I didn't know if it would be okay to help myself. Gregor had twisted my world, and I didn't know how to act properly.

A small shrub had been planted in a shiny black pot beside the sunny window. Dark green leaves swayed under the vent. It appeared livelier than anyone at the table.

I jumped when the door opened. A pudgy man with a sneer walked in carrying a thick folio. "Let's make this quick. Jay Convery, ASA, 1st Circuit." His tone, both annoyed and arrogant, didn't fit his gait or oily face. He puffed out pale cheeks and dropped into a seat across from Edward as Bill introduced everyone.

Deanna sat stiffly, but I could tell she wanted to talk. I wanted to know how Gregor had manipulated this man to do his bidding, but I couldn't hint at my part in this.

Jay Convery handed Bill a paper. "The charges recommended are for material support for a designated foreign terrorist organization, namely the Islamic State group."

I flushed angrily at the man's arrogant expression and tone, which implied some pleasure at being involved. If he worked directly for Gregor, I could only hope to meet him with Nightarmor.

I wouldn't have understood the importance of his statement, if it weren't for Deanna's outburst. "Tyler wouldn't. You can't have any evidence! If you did, we'd be in a federal office."

"Your degree is psychology, not law, is it not, Ms. Ramnath?" He wore a sneer and leaned back in a more relaxed pose.

"She is not wrong. What evidence do you have, Mr. Convery?" Edward asked.

"You'll get your chance for discovery when we move forward on this."

Lie. Flustered and excited, I tapped my pad twice. I glowered and had to focus on the dark leaves dancing beside the window.

Bill scratched a note and showed it to Edward.

It took a moment before the New York lawyer asked, "Do you have evidence?"

Jay eyes flicked to the side and he straightened. "Of course," he lied. "Why would I waste our time if I did not?"

I tapped my pad twice with a frown. Unsure before, I knew he had brought us here because Gregor had persuaded him to do so. The Upre had paid him, most likely, all so that Gregor could send me threats by text. My pulse pounded in my ears. I glared at the man.

"You are holding Tyler on the basis of this evidence?" Edward asked.

"Yes, until we decide if we are to move this to Federal."

Still a lie. I tapped my pencil. I had never understood the Tallahassee legal system, but accepted that it had to have some level of fairness. Beyond Gregor and whatever he had engineered, this seemed like a horrible system if they didn't need to prove someone was guilty.

Deanna's family attorney tilted his head and nodded. "Then, there is no racial bias or profiling, considering the Ramnath's Indian ancestry?"

"What? No." Jay's hands dropped from the table to his lap.

True. I tapped once, not understanding the question myself.

"Then you have evidence and a chain of custody dated prior to Tyler Ramnath's arrest that you will provide during discovery?"

I felt lost, and the state's attorney looked flustered. What had I missed?

"Of course."

Lie. I tapped twice.

Bill started to scribble, but Edward continued. "You do understand that lacking a proper chain of evidence, which we would investigate thoroughly, we would counter with a hate crime against you personally, looking not just for your removal from office but an indictment. Any fabrication of evidence after this point would come into question under that investigation."

Jay Convery blanched even paler. "If we chose to not move forward . . . ?"

From one of his folios, Edward pulled papers bound by a silver clip. "If we leave this meeting without Tyler Ramnath's release, I'll walk right over and file."

The arrogance left the man Gregor had set against Tyler and me. Jay stared at the pages held in the air as if they might be a viper. "I . . ."

Edward placed the pages carefully on the table and pulled a thicker wad out. "This is for civil court."

Beyond the papers slowly waving in the air, Deanna wore a cruel smile. My heart leaped. Somehow, though I understood none of it, we were going to free Tyler.

Jay Convery stood fiddling with a middle button of his suit. "I would prefer to consolidate the evidence and refine my case, in any course of action. The investigation is not over, but Tyler Ramnath will be released." He lied, and his fingers were shaking.

I wanted to stand and felt like I could float, but tapped the pad twice. Quietly, Bill reached over and stilled my pen without glancing at me.

Edward stood as the pudgy man skittered to the door. When I tried to confirm that Tyler was free, Bill gestured for me to be quiet. I ended up leaving the building with him while Deanna and Edward took a few minutes longer.

Outside, I burst. "Tyler's free?"

Bill rested a hand on my shoulder and chuckled. "Yes. It doesn't sound like they have anything. I wouldn't have guessed it and don't really understand."

My bouncing joy stopped, and I looked away to the embellished church. Edward had foiled Gregor's plan, with my help, but I doubted this would be the end of it. I didn't know enough to even guess how he might attack next.

He knew how to hurt me, though. Blood drained from my face. Tyler wasn't safe, and I'd have to explain the threat so they could prepare.

Deanna's voice trailed out of the door, and I peered at her happy expression. Who was the next friend that Gregor would go after? As they reached us, she smiled at me, and the worry lifted. For the moment, we had saved Tyler.

Edward Miller nodded to Bill, then studied me. "Pleasure to meet you, Ahnjii Fate." He likely had understood what Bill and I had been doing.

"Thank you for getting Tyler released." I couldn't help but grin like an idiot.

"Call me Ted."

"Thank you, Ted."

CHAPTER 12

THE SUN HAD RISEN straight above before they released Tyler. Deanna whisked us off to the airport as if Jay Convery might change his mind. The reek of petroleum and asphalt hung in the air when Gregor messaged me again. "THIS ISN'T OVER."

Neatly trimmed shrubs grew out of white gravel in front of a small building that hired out private jets. A driver in a blue suit unloaded Deanna's suitcases onto a golden cart. She held onto Tyler as they walked through the glass doors into the building.

"I KNOW." I didn't know what else to reply. Gloating or threatening wouldn't help. I still hadn't had a moment to talk to Tyler. Why had I even replied?

"Ahnjii, c'mon." Deanna let the door close behind her.

The driver rolled down the sidewalk toward me. A stray piece of gravel shot out from under the cart's wheel, and luggage tilted. The flowered bag which Doris had lent me didn't budge.

I walked to the door ahead of the man, stepped inside, and held it open. Flicking the ends of my braid, I forced a smile when he thanked me. What was I going to do about Gregor?

I'd missed my chance to talk with Shailagh, but she was more worried about Clarita and the wildlings. I could tell she'd been annoyed when I tried to send her the reason I left for Pensacola. She didn't even know that I was on my way back.

Three cups of water out of the cooler, and we were boarding the small plane. The same type of vehicle had looked so big when I first came to Earth. I wanted to explain to Tyler privately what had happened, but the seats were too close together.

Deanna bubbled with laughter. "We're going to celebrate. Champagne."

One of the attendants had already poured a clear drink into her glass. He smiled at her excitement. "Good news?" he asked.

She pointed her tall glass at Tyler. "We're going home."

Tyler smiled, but they seemed reserved, as if the experience had numbed them.

"You okay?" I asked, clicking my harness on.

"Better." Tyler took a tall glass of Deanna's champagne, but didn't drink.

I caused this. My chest tightened. "I'm happy we're going home." I grimaced at the taste of Deanna's celebratory beverage. Perhaps they had tea.

Tyler tapped absently on their glass. "I'm grateful to be out of there, but I don't understand."

"What?"

"Any of it. I could see if I were one of the organizers, or even someone important to the protest, but I wasn't. I've checked with the others, and no one else has been arrested. Not one."

I took another sip, shivered, and stared at the rising bubbles. They clung to the sides as if fearful, but eventual they lost their grip and popped on the surface. Tyler needed to know what had happened and why.

My opportunity didn't come until later that afternoon when Deanna took a call with their parents. I motioned for Tyler to follow me out to the pool.

The chilly breeze drifted across the pool, forming ripples. A bee buzzed past us. Cars rumbled outside the neighborhood.

Taking a deep breath, I stared at the water. "This is my fault," I said.

Tyler had changed into a black shirt with sleeves so long they draped over their hands. "No, it's not." Their gesture rustled the cuffs.

I turned to face them, grabbed my braid, and relayed my experience with Gregor, starting from the beginning. Without detailing my sources, I explained what I understood about the Upre. I brought up the messages on my phone. "I'm hoping Gregor's threats do not include you anymore, but I wanted to warn you."

Tyler swore. "Vampires now? What else?"

"I'm sorry."

"This isn't your fault. This Gregor didn't warn you who he would target." Tyler dropped into one of the chairs. "I'll be careful." They tapped a quick beat on the arm of the chair. "What are you going to do?"

"I'm going to talk to Shailagh and see if she has any ideas." I wanted to track Gregor down and kill him. If I were on Duruce, the Queen would have me remove any such threat. "Do you have any thoughts?" I needed someone who understood power and politics.

Tyler shook their head slowly. "Gregor Gehrke? I'll search for the name. What else is out there?"

The question wasn't directed at me, but I couldn't tell him about the Nedjir. After the trouble with the wight, I had asked Laura about it. Tyler knew about everything else and hadn't caused any trouble. She had convinced me that it was best not to disclose anything about her people.

Tyler jumped up. "Let's skate. Helps me think."

"I want to check on Woo. Tonight?" I wasn't about to mention my concern over the wildling in my back parking lot and leaving Woo alone. On the ride to the airport, I'd texted Laura that Tyler was safe and I'd be home to cook dinner.

Tyler nodded, then tilted their head. "Nobody knows where Woo came from? None of your cryptid friends? Where did they come from?"

I fingered the sharp post of Shailagh's earring. Nightarmor formed a clip which pressed the metal ball against my ear. "I don't know." My focus had to be protecting my friends from Gregor, and I had no idea how to do that. I had to hope that Shailagh would have some advice. I sent her a thought through the sigils pressed against my earlobe, and felt the odd flow. *Back home.*

Tyler hugged me before heading for the house. "Let me know about tonight."

"I love you. I'm glad you're okay." I still felt responsible.

"Love you, too."

I strode toward the gate. The children next door were calling out to each other in playful, excited voices. I should be happy too. Tyler was home. I couldn't get Gregor's last message out of my head.

Shailagh sent an image of the Lichgate tree. *Meet me.* I could sense that it would be a while before she'd be there.

There was enough time for me to feed Woo and head to the tree.

I passed through the gate and began the jog home. I'd left the flowery bag from Doris behind, but could pick it up tonight. *Shailagh has to have an answer.*

CHAPTER 13

I slowed to a walk when I spotted the figure sitting in the blue sedan opposite my apartment building. The car had an odd shape with a long hood that led to a steeply sloping window.

Khimmer, wildlings?

None, Mistress.

The blue paint had faded in spots, and there were dents on the door that I recognized.

Darren McGyver, Knight of something and a witch, opened his door and held his straw fedora atop light brown hair as he stepped out.

My pulse quickened. Mrs. Forster hadn't come out, and the flamingos stood alone in front of my apartment. I veered across the street to meet him. His hair looked disheveled, and he squinted despite the shade of his brim.

"What are you doing here?" The last time we'd talked, he'd been concerned that Tyler wouldn't keep quiet about the wight. I'd taken it as a threat. Gregor having Tyler arrested was bad enough.

Darren closed his car door with a grinding thud and studied me. "Everything okay?"

What did he know? Was he here over the whole wight thing, or Gregor? I didn't trust the man, and Shailagh had been clear about avoiding him. He wore the same brown leather jacket as before. It wasn't that cold. "Great. What do you want?"

Darren adjusted his hat and forced a smile that didn't fit his face. "I thought we could talk. Coffee? I know a restaurant that makes a fantastic Reuben. They make the dressing from scratch."

I started to relax, but didn't want him around when Shailagh arrived. She didn't get along with the man, and I needed her help. "No thanks. I'm busy."

"I imagine you are." His tone was smug.

He spoke the truth, so I doubted this was about me killing the wight, or about Tyler and John's involvement. How would he know about Gregor? His Knight organization supposedly kept an eye on human and cryptid interaction so that humans wouldn't find out and panic. Why would he care about an Upre pressuring me to sign a contract? He wouldn't. It sounded like common practice with witches.

"I don't have time for your games." I nodded my head toward my apartment. "I'm making dinner. Leave."

"I want to help."

Truth. I hesitated, shuffling in place. Any help with Gregor would be welcome, but I didn't trust his motives. He might even be here about Clarita. I didn't know. If Shailagh couldn't help, I still had his card. "No, thanks."

"Listen, I just . . ."

"Leave." Angry at Gregor and myself, my tone came out too strong. I took a breath. "Just leave."

He frowned, nodded, and pulled out another of his sigil-masked Knight cards to hand to me. It just reminded me of how he'd tricked me before. I took it, and a flush came up my neck.

As I ran for my apartment, Darren called after me, "Be careful, Ahnjii Fate."

Under my breath I groaned at the sight of Mrs. Forster coming out with her broom. *Damn me to Hades.* Darren's door screeched closed as I took the steps two at a time. Had I made a mistake? My fingers pinched his card. If Shailagh couldn't help me come up with a plan, I'd call him. I needed to hurry and meet her at the Lichgate tree.

Woo WHISTLED at me as I headed for the door. I'd barely taken time to grab a handful of pistachios for them and a drink of water for myself.

"Sorry. I'll be back tonight."

Darren's car was gone, and I had begun to believe I'd been rash. I might call even after meeting with Shailagh. He and his Knights might have a better understanding of the world of power and politics than either I or Shailagh might.

The sun had started to drop comfortably toward the horizon as I jogged toward Lichgate. I'd worried that I might be late after dealing with Darren, but I hadn't heard from Shailagh yet.

When I turned off the road, the dirt parking lot was empty, as usual. Few came to visit the tree. Flowers blossomed near the path with a fragrant sweet scent. I had barely started down the path when some of the giant tree came into view and a portal lit between the brush.

I arrived as the portal light was fading and Shailagh walked toward me. Squirrels chided us from a nearby perch. The long branches of the Lichgate tree that rested on the ground melded into the dark grass under the shade of the forest.

Shailagh's face was tight. "Idin will be meeting us here."

"Idin?" After I'd asked the question, I remembered the name. The high Fae who would be questioning me about the wight. I hadn't planned on that.

"Then I should be quick. I believe I've pissed off that Upre even more." I explained what had happened to Tyler, how we freed him, and even offered to show her the texts, but she waved me off. "I don't know how to deal with Gregor."

She frowned and spoke with harsh voice. "You'll need to leave. Hide. The Upre are known to leverage friends and family in their business dealings. However, this is extreme, even for them. Usually they use enticements rather than threats. I have not asked about Gregor, but I will."

"I can't leave." My first reaction caught my breath. Was I willing to sacrifice Tyler?

I'd hoped she'd have better advice than Laura, at least something more accommodating than losing everything I cared about. The breeze rustled leaves overhead and carried the scent of blossoms. Behind Shailagh, small ferns grew off one of the leaning branches of Lichgate. Like tiny green feathers, they swayed in unison. I couldn't leave.

Wildling, Mistress.

I blinked and peered around with quick snaps of my head. *I don't see anything.*

Approaching through the woods to your left, Mistress. In human form. Two now.

"We've got company," I said to Shailagh.

There are six, Mistress. Surrounding you.

I didn't want to kill another of them.

Full armor. Dory, I thought to Khimmer.

Nightarmor poured over me. As I saw the wildlings through Khimmer's vision, the shapes leaping through the brush and trees turned from orange to near red. They were shifting. I reached up and grabbed the butt of the spear. My heart began to pound. After all the frustration Gregor caused, an actual skirmish had me excited.

The shining black dory stood higher than my head; on the butt it had a dull point, and at the tip a sharp spade-shaped blade.

Shailagh stalked toward the forest between us and the parking lot. Her fingers pointed at the ground, and the trees there stiffened and their limbs bent down. I scrambled to cover her back with both hands on my weapon. The wildlings couldn't hurt me through Nightarmor, no matter how strong they were. Nails and teeth were no match for metal.

The wildlings paced their attack perfectly, each arriving from a different direction and converging on me. In their shifted form they were shaggy creatures. Their blunt muzzles shortened their noses and exposed sharp teeth. They did not look canine or any other form of animal, just beasts.

Only one swerved toward Shailagh.

Using the dull butt, I dove toward the largest of the wildlings. He jerked aside, so I caught him with a glancing blow across the temple. It sent him staggering to his knees. Recoiling, I jabbed low behind me and stabbed into flesh with the sharp tip where I could be sure I didn't aim for throat or heart.

I utilized the impact to leap forward into the space the largest male had left open, spun, and slid my grip down to extend the reach of the dory and leave the wildling pinned. Space and keeping them to the front of me would give me an advantage. My pulse raced. I grinned under my helmet. It would still be a challenge, made unfair with Nightarmor.

It was a female who reached oversized claws toward the tip of my weapon embedded in her thigh. With a twist, I slid it sideways out of her leg and across the chest of the male beside her. They both howled.

A deep gash opened in his flesh, and he stumbled back into a third wildling's leap. I appreciated an attacker I could face. The thought of Gregor had me snarling.

Shailagh had moved deeper into the woods to my right, becoming a vague orange shape fighting a darker red wildling.

A quick step to the side, and I caught the leaping wildling with the dull butt in his temple. I cringed at the strike, fearing I'd broken bone. I still didn't want to kill any of them.

Clarita was not among those who attacked me. Either she focused on Shailagh or wasn't here.

Shailagh? I asked Khimmer

Keeping her distance from her attacker, Mistress. They are focused on you.

Got that.

I dodged the last wildling with a quick dip to her side.

Claws scraped against Nightarmor's boot. A strong grip tried to yank my stance out from under me. The largest wildling bled from his temple, but had managed to get to his knees too quickly. I jabbed the sharp tip deep into his forearm.

I couldn't shift when the wildling who I'd stabbed in the thigh leaped for me. With my weapon pinned in his arm and leg still holding, I went down under her weight.

I let go of the dory, and it melted in a stream into my gauntlet.

Short blade.

Yes, Mistress.

Nightarmor shifted on my left vambrace, and I reached for the hilt. Strong claws grabbed both of my arms, and a foot or knee pressed on my back.

"I don't want to kill you." My voice, more like a growl, echoed loudly in my helmet.

With a dizzying whirl, the two wildlings lifted me off the ground. I dug metal heels into shins and knees. I elicited grunts and snarls with my attempts, but they didn't let me go.

Spikes, I thought to Khimmer. I shouldn't risk more wildling deaths, but I had let them catch me by being too careful. You would have thought the Aegis monks had beat any mercy out of me by now.

Yes, Mistress.

One of the wildlings howled. Their voice was thick in their shifted forms. "Cowardly witch." One shifted their grip, but neither lessened their hold, and my feet still dangled.

A third had reached me and locked my right arm even more. What was happening to Shailagh that she did not help me? I could have Khimmer make spikes longer and thinner, like those I'd used to kill the wight. My nose wrinkled with an angry grimace. Somewhere distant, a vehicle started and revved its engine. Perhaps a witness would come, and they'd leave. Would they kill an innocent human? I couldn't let them.

My pulse pounded in my ears. "Let me go now, or I'll send you to Hades." I had never accepted being restrained. If need be, I would resort to becoming a porcupine. Wildlings might die.

Metal scraped against my helmet. In Khimmer's vision,

I caught only a dark band. A long squeak sounded behind my neck that sent a chill up my spine.

Khimmer?

They have tied a metal cable around your neck, Mistress.

Nightarmor would protect my bones and flesh, but I did not like being restrained even further. I thrashed in anger, and one wildling laughed.

With a voice thick in beast form, a male said, "We'll see how you do against tires."

A second voice, a female, spoke clearer on the other side. "If that doesn't crush you, how long can you last under water?"

I would not last long under water, Khimmer had made that clear. Shailagh had her own troubles, obviously. I had to get out of this.

Porcupine into them.

Nightarmor adjusted across my back. The wildlings holding me burst into a cacophony of screams and howls. I shifted forward from Nightarmor's piercings, then dropped. The drag of the cable at my throat made me stagger backward to keep my balance.

Retract spikes. Sword. I would not be restrained.

As I reached to grab the hilt, a wildling barked three times. I pulled Nightarmor's sword with my right hand and reached back with my left to the cable clasped behind my neck. Khimmer had retracted the spikes, so the weapon moved freely and nothing hampered my left-handed search. Through the helmet, the wildlings were colored shades of hot red scrambling away from me. Closer to the tree, I caught the movement that could be Shailagh with her own troublesome wildling.

Can I cut this? Turning, I raised my sword.

Yes, Mistress.

Before I could process Khimmer's thought and respond, the cable went taut. It jerked me off my feet and slammed me onto my back as it dragged me through the grass. I struggled with my left hand still on the cable. Branches snapped, and leaves crumbled under me. The canopy above rolled slowly along, despite how fast I sped head first on my back.

The engine I'd heard earlier revved again. I was being dragged toward it and slashed weakly at the cable behind me. Would they really drive over me? I needed my legs and sword pointed in the direction of the threat.

Can Nightarmor survive a car's weight? They'd warned me against getting crushed before.

Unlikely, Mistress.

I needed to spin feet first. My path met a tree trunk which my shoulder slammed into. The impact nearly flipped me, and my legs swung. Larger trees and thin brush flew past. The joints and ridges of Nightarmor dug into the soil and straightened me. Gritting my teeth, I reached as high as I could on the cable.

Back shield. I needed less resistance and imagined the shallow bowl I wanted.

I felt Nightarmor reshaping from my shoulders to hips and raised my heels. My right elbow lifted up as the smooth, convex shield formed under me. The curved surface below me easily slid side to side through brush and debris.

A second engine revved near the first. They were close.

Straining, I pulled on the cable and felt my sled shift. I could do this. A second tree slammed into my left side, jarring my elbow and flipping me helmet first into the leaves. I could hear only my pounding pulse and sloughing debris for a second. The impact had skidded me sideways as well, and the drag readjusted me.

I would make an easy target, face down in my turtle

shell. Pressing my knees and right forearm into the ground stretched muscles despite Nightarmor. Throwing a hip to my rear, I flipped Nightarmor's sled.

The engines were close. Tires crunched through leaves.

I yelled, pulling hard with my left hand. I was not going to die tonight. My sled spun.

A blocky shape revved in the parking lot, its headlights off. The cable ran to a box on the front of it. A larger truck rolled forward from my side. They each had a dull orange driver sitting inside, wildlings in human form.

I slashed with Nightarmor's blade; it seemed a hand's width longer than usual, and blue sparks flew off the cable just beyond my left hand. The strike had been too soon and didn't sever.

The large truck with oversized wheels roared and raced toward me but aimed for just in front of the other vehicle. My new angle gave me a better grip with my left hand, and I pulled strained muscles until the cable ran beside my legs and arced up to the vehicle ahead. I assumed Khimmer would not allow me to cut through Nightarmor.

My blade sliced the cable, and it snapped across the hood of the blocky shape ahead, whipped across the roof, and shattered the windshield. I flipped up on my heels, but too much momentum threw me toward the oncoming truck.

Remove shield.

Yes, Mistress.

The fat front tires sped at my back. Dirt flew from the rear. I didn't intend to die in a parking lot.

Full climbing nails. "Damn me to Hades," I growled as I sprang for the bumper.

CHAPTER 15

WHEN I SLAMMED onto the front of the speeding truck, the impact hurt, but not as badly as when John had hit me with the van in Slovenia. I still lost my blade, vaguely aware of it turning liquid once separated from me. Metal screeching echoed in my helmet, louder than the blood pounding in my ears. I held on with gauntlet nails dug into the hood and bumper. My left knee shifted up, and I rode the hood of their truck. "I'm not going to kill them," I promised myself through gritted teeth.

My left side ached at every joint and rib. I'd climbed high enough that I could see the wildling clearly in his human form. Glowing orange in Khimmer's vision, a young man with a curly stubble on his chin pulled back from the window with his eyebrows raised in surprise. A fleck of bright red glinted in his eye. The gray sky flashed a reflection across the glass, a faint image of the canopy above. The engine smelled hot.

I never saw the tree we hit. The wildling driver looked as shocked as I was when I flew off his hood. The momentum slammed his forehead into the steering wheel in a blur.

My right heel caught the tree mid-air. The world spun with a passing glimpse of dark red shapes, but I had no true orientation. They could have been the wildings left back by the tree or new arrivals. Even knowing Nightarmor would protect me upon landing, my heart leaped in my chest.

Brush tangled around me, foiling my spin and leaving me to land on knees and gauntlets. Uncontrolled, I rolled to slap my back against a small tree and staggered to my feet. The world still spun, but the wildlings were mainly to my left, with only two left in the parking lot ahead of me.

Trees creaked near the group of wildlings. Assuming I'd been taken care of by the truck, the rest of the pack must have turned their focus on Shailagh. I wasn't going to let them harm her.

Dory.

Yes, Mistress.

My first two steps were off mark and wobbly, but I picked up speed. The spear had barely formed when I pulled it off my back and held it tucked along my vambrace past my elbow, trailing behind me. I crushed and tore through brush and vines, making for the lighter shade of orange that I guessed to be Shailagh. *Hades.* My face flushed and pulse pounded. Still not intending to kill any more wildlings, I planned on a few having to be carried away.

There were four actively trying to reach Shailagh, one hanging tangled in the air, and two others lying on the ground where I'd left them by the Lichgate tree. The limbs that slapped out of the woods to knock aside wildlings reminded me of the wight. High Fae magic seemed formidable, but the wildings were resilient and persistent.

As I rounded toward a wildling, the Lichgate tree glowed with an intense white light. I'd never seen it through Khimmer's vision.

Partially blinded, I thrust into the side of the closest wildling's knee with the sharp tip. A female howled as I pierced through cartilage to bone. Khimmer had to reshape as the blade stuck.

A shape darkened the portal, but I had a wildling breaking off their attack on Shailagh to leap at me. Positioned as I was, it would have been easy to thrust into their upper body, but it might have been a killing blow. Teeth grinding, I stepped back and swung the butt of the dory into the side of their head. Their left forearm took some of the impact, but the strike rattled the spear against my gauntleted fingers.

I jumped clear as they hit the ground with a dull thud. Two wildlings were down.

The shape at the tree resolved into a squat male shadow.

Another wildling howled as Shailagh yanked him into the air with a tangle of vines.

As if on cue from the new arrival, the attack disintegrated. Shifted wildlings dragged away some of those I'd disabled, and Shailagh released one to land between us and the tree. Branches rustled back into place around me.

When Shailagh released the second wildling to drop to their feet, I recognized the voice. "Witch," Clarita said as she turned red eyes on me.

I let out a hot breath inside my helmet and side stepped toward Shailagh. "Are you okay?"

She swore, "Nails." One of the wildlings had gotten a swipe from her collarbone, across her armpit, and down her bicep. Her shirt had torn open, and blood matted what was left.

I thought she watched the wildlings leave, but she peered at the approaching man. A high Fae with telltale ears poking over his hair, he had two nubs of bone protruding at his hairline. He glared from us to the retreating wildlings.

Remove helmet.

Yes, Mistress.

"Liam's lips, Shailagh. What have you done?" His hair was a dark red, the color of drying blood. I stared at the horns, reminded of a demon from one of Tyler's manga. He walked toward us in a pair of black jeans and sharp-toed boots. "Obviously, this is the witch who's causing all the problems?"

I blinked and started to respond, but Shailagh gestured me silent. "Yes, Idin. This is Ahnjii."

"Don't speak for her." His black shirt had gray embroidery on it.

Hot and bruised, I wanted to remove my armor but thought better of it. Shailagh had made it clear that her people might have an unhealthy interest in Nightarmor. I propped myself on my dory with one hand and hoped he hadn't noticed my missing helmet. Looking as innocent as I could, I slid my other hand behind my back.

Form helmet in my hand.

Yes, Mistress.

Metal pushed between my fingertips, and I felt the weight of the helmet. "Hi," I said. Shailagh needed to get her wound looked at.

Idin snorted and rubbed one of his nubs. "Don't 'hi' me. We've got so much of a mess that we can only hope the other wildling packs don't join in and turn it into a full-scale war. Nails, do you have any idea what you've caused?"

Perhaps it was the previous warning, or the way he spoke to Shailagh, but I didn't like this high Fae. For her sake, I spoke politely. "I hadn't intended to start trouble."

"You killed a wildling. What did you think would happen?"

I studied Idin. Men like this often would berate no matter the response. I wanted answers about how to deal with Clarita, more so about Gregor, but I doubted Idin had anything useful to offer.

When I didn't answer, he huffed and gestured toward the retreating wildlings. "What do you think will happen after today's mishap?"

"Mishap?" I asked. "Would you rather we both died? They attacked us with every intent on killing at least me."

Idin didn't drop his eyes. "Might have been better that way."

"We're going to have company soon." Shailagh held her wound. "Someone had to have heard all this."

Growling, Idin waved off her comment. "I came here to determine if this witch could be as violent as you described — if she could in fact be responsible for the present hostilities with Clarita's clan." He motioned in the direction the wildlings had left. "I've got my answer. This disaster only makes the situation worse."

I still burned on Idin's comment that we should have died. "I'm not going to die so that Clarita can hold onto her clan."

"Perhaps." He turned from me to address Shailagh. "You are right. We should go. The Council will want to hear of these latest developments."

Shailagh nodded while glancing at me. "Be careful, Ahnjii."

They strode toward the Lichgate tree, and I sighed. The attack and our defense didn't seem to be making Shailagh's situation any better. I'd hoped to get her advice on Gregor, but that wouldn't be happening. After the intensity of the battle, I felt adrift. Beyond their footsteps through the leaves, I could hear dogs barking and a man's voice, cars on the road, and distant sirens.

The portal opened with a bright slice of light down the trunk, and their two shadows stepped inside. Alone, I had no new answers to my trouble with Gregor and had likely hardened Clarita's resolve. I took a deep breath.

Remove armor.

Yes, Mistress.

Sweating trickling down my neck, I headed toward the road for home.

IN THE PARKING LOT, THE WILDLINGS' truck had its hood crumpled against the tree. The cool air drew off some of my sweat and brought the sharp scent of petroleum. Sirens were getting closer and sounded like baying dogs. The other vehicle was gone. I'd never heard it leave.

Voices were coming from the woods in the direction of the tree. There were homes nearby. Our skirmish had likely made a bit of noise. I stepped onto the roadside with bruised ribs and without answers. My step was none too lively.

A beat up blue car pulled off the road ahead of me and waited. I could make out Darren's straw hat through the windows. The police passed us with their sirens blaring and pulled into Lichgate park.

"Damn me to Hades." I was in no mood for his games. Swerving, I walked deeper into the grass, avoiding the side of the car where he sat.

He leaned over to the passenger side and wound a crank to lower a window. As I approached, he was stretched across his seats, one hand on the steering wheel and the other leaning on the passenger seat. He offered a false smile. "Need a ride?"

"No thanks." I kept walking, though the grass grew higher and the angle pitched.

A car honked as Darren started to drive on the roadside to keep pace with me. "Trouble? We really should talk."

"Leave me alone."

We were approaching a mailbox, but he kept rolling along beside me. "I could meet you back at your apartment, if you'd prefer. But you look a little worn."

The ground angled up at the drive ahead, a short obstacle but I did feel tired, and Darren seemed insistent on talking. The cars buzzed past. The breeze brought the scent of someone cooking on a grill. The police sirens had stopped. A bird landed on the mailbox, then lit off as if annoyed with our approach.

I stopped, staring at the grass at my feet. "What do you want?"

"To help. We need to talk about Clarita, before this reaches the humans."

My side throbbed, thigh and ribs. I was thirsty and growing hungry. I didn't trust Darren, nor particularly like him, but he was a witch who might have some advice that a high Fae wouldn't. Could I ask him about Gregor and the Upre? "Drive me home, then leave me alone?"

"Save you a walk. You're getting a bruise on your leg."

I flicked to see the black and purple emerging from under the bottom of my shorts. "Okay." My tone belied my actual interest in what Darren might have to say. He knew about Clarita. Did he know about Gregor? I didn't feel comfortable inviting him into the situation, but if he offered information, I would take it.

The car smelled like stale food that reminded me of

Tyler's. Other than that, it looked like the old car that Laura drove. The dash under the front window had cracked and leaked a yellow fiber. The rugs looked matted and worn. The harness was little more than a belt.

Darren wrestled a black knob attached to a lever that disappeared into the bottom of the car. "Has Clarita approached you yet?"

So, he had no idea about the attack that just occurred. "Yes, she wants to kill me."

The car made a grinding noise, then he sped off the grass. "And the high Fae, Shailagh. She thinks it will help her keep her position. She's wrong. Samuel is biding his time, but we believe he will regain his control of the pack."

I hadn't considered Samuel since our dealings with the rogue. Had I considered him dead? "So I just wait it out?"

Darren snorted. "From a distance. They've scouted out your apartment. Disappear for a bit. I can let you know when it's safe."

My jaw tightened, though he'd given me the same advice as Laura and Shailagh. I didn't want to leave my new friends. "Why would you want to help me?"

"The bloody kind of bodies that the wildlings leave are no fun to hide. If it becomes public, then we risk someone tying it to previous leaks. It just feeds the conspiracies."

I laughed. "You're concerned my corpse will be hard to explain?"

Darren tilted his head, eyes on the road. "Yes. I'm sure you're a very nice person besides."

He didn't seem to know about Gregor, and I didn't intend to bring him up. Getting turned into a host likely wouldn't be a concern for him as long as it didn't come up on the internet. Perhaps Tyler being threatened would be of interest, but I didn't trust Darren's solutions.

"I appreciate your advice."

We drove into College Town past the green sports field. "But, you're not going to take it?"

"I have to think about it."

"Clarita will move quickly."

She already had. I needed a quiet moment with Woo, some tea, and perhaps some noodles. A bath would be nice. The ride with Darren hadn't given me any answers except about Samuel, though it didn't seem helpful.

My phone buzzed, and I retrieved it from my shorts. I winced at the bruise Clarita's people had left me.

Tyler texted, "Skate?"

I smiled. My ribs hurt, but the simple exertion to some music would be welcome. "Yes," I texted. Maybe I could forget about Gregor and Clarita for a few minutes.

CHAPTER 17

THE SUN still hung too high when I reached the large gym that Tyler and Deanna used as a skating rink. The wood floor had a taped oval around the outer edge, but otherwise they kept it clear. The air hung quiet and chilly with a hint of bearing grease. Deanna had had a dance in it once, before I'd arrived on Earth.

Tyler sat on the floor lacing their skates while my bag and two water bottles waited at the doorway. Dark shadows hung under their eyes. "Bee Gees?"

I rolled my eyes and dropped down by my bag. The remote for the music was beside it. "Queen. We'll work our way there." We had a song list we'd worked out a long time ago.

Remove boots.

Yes, Mistress.

Nightarmor melted into two anklets wide enough to fit above my skates. Khimmer had the routine memorized after all the time Tyler and I had spent on the floor. "It's been a while."

"I've missed it." Tyler tapped their wheels on the floor.

"I need this." They peered at me. "Everything okay?"

"I just want to have some fun." I laughed, hoping it sounded lighter than I felt. "I'll whine about things later." Tyler didn't need to worry about Clarita at the moment.

I turned the music on, and lights sparkled colorfully across the walls and floor. Tyler took off for a lap while I finished lacing.

Skating in rhythm with Tyler brought back a comfortable peace. We didn't say much, possibly because we didn't want to bring up darker subjects. Most of the time we commented on the music or laughed when I couldn't keep up with Tyler's more complicated steps.

It was the release I needed. The room, lights, and music spun around me, and my ribs barely hurt. I loved the times we had in their gym.

I'd hidden the Blessed Blade here until I'd try and find a way home again. A crawl space ran underneath with a few blocks of concrete loosely placed in an opening. Dark, cramped, and crawling with insects, it seemed a good place to hide Nyx's weapon. Perhaps I could persuade Deanna to let me search for the way home again. Returning to my duty on Duruce was one way to keep Tyler safe, unless Gregor took his revenge in my absence.

Tyler noticed my expression and pointed toward the corner where our water waited. I skidded in behind them and slid down the wall to the floor. "This is great," I said. We'd gone through our favorite play list and moved on to a second.

"You've got a text." Tyler handed me my water. "Later?"

I gestured toward my phone while I drank. They slid the phone across the floor.

I recognized Gregor's number.

CHAPTER 18

I PUT down the water bottle, wiped my hands on my shorts, and picked up my phone. I smelled slightly rank after the skirmish with the wildlings while wearing full armor. As they drank, Tyler studied me with dark eyes over their purple container.

I read Gregor's text. "I MISJUDGED YOUR WILLINGNESS TO USE YOUR ABILITIES AT THE PROCEEDINGS YESTERDAY. I SHOULD HAVE CONSIDERED THE POSSIBILITY. IF THE ABILITIES FOR WHICH YOU ARE EMPLOYED WERE TO BECOME MORE WIDELY KNOWN, THE MEDIA WOULD MAKE YOUR LIFE QUITE INTOLERABLE. NOT TO MENTION CERTAIN RESEARCH COMPANIES AND GOVERNMENTAL AGENCIES. WHATEVER LIFE YOU CLING TO PRESENTLY WOULD NO LONGER EXIST."

The ache in my ribs reasserted itself. Other than plunging my life into chaos, I saw little benefit to Gregor's ploy. If he destroyed what ties I had to Tallahassee, wouldn't that prompt me to do exactly what Laura suggested and disappear? Perhaps he hadn't considered that. Despite his supposed resources, Gregor did not appear to have the same guile that others such as Gigina had had.

"What have you learned of Gregor?" I asked Tyler without looking up.

They sighed. "Not much. There are a couple men by that name in Europe, more by the name of Greg, including some who live here in America. I've created some lists and begun tracking some of the more affluent. White male, tall, fit — rich. Nearly all meet your description, though many have facial hair, but that's no solid indication. Even weight has to be suspect unless it is a recent data point. I took a break to skate, but I don't have anything definitive to offer."

Gregor's threat didn't appear as weighted as having Tyler arrested, but it did lead to a result I didn't want: I would lose my friends. Laura, Shailagh, and even Darren had suggested it, but I couldn't bring myself to accept leaving everything and everyone I'd grown to love. I was too selfish.

Even if Tyler did find exactly the Gregor Gehrke that I wanted, what would I do, assassinate him?

Tyler gestured to my phone. "Is that him?"

I nodded sullenly and handed it over. Tyler read quietly. The joy of skating had been burned out of me with reality crushing in. Yanking laces out, I began removing my skates. The music seemed annoying.

"He doesn't seem very adept at his persuasion. My arrest was a far more effective pressure than this. If he follows through with it, everybody loses." Tyler started to say something, stopped, and pushed the phone back to me. "I'm having a hard time with all of this. Cryptids have existed all this time around us, and I spent an inordinate amount of time researching. Yes, there have been those who claim shifters, Bigfoot, Fae, and vampires exist, and as many disprove their evidence.

"Woo. Nobody seems to know where they're from. I can't shake this hole in my stomach knowing that this has been around me all this time. That they kidnapped and changed John; he still doesn't seem quite right. That they're after you for your abilities. Your truthsense. Your armor. Your world. Humans on a tidally locked planet that has a wee gate that you came through."

Tyler's mouth opened to continue and they snapped it shut. With slow movements, they began unlacing their skates as if they worked in a dream. I felt like I'd broken them. Maybe it would be best if I disappeared.

"I'm sorry."

Tyler snorted. "Don't be. I want to know, even if some aspects terrify me. The parts you won't tell me hang like a weight, though I understand."

I hadn't told Tyler about the Nedjir as Laura continued to ask me not to. "There's just one thing, and it is not dangerous at all." And Khimmer. "What do you think I should do?" I pointed at the now dark phone.

Tyler kicked off a skate. "Over that? Nothing. He's got to realize the consequences of following through with his threat; later, if not when he wrote it."

I wasn't sure. Tyler's search for Gregor appeared to be taking more time than I wanted to wait. Shailagh would be tied up with Idin and their Council. I could try contacting her later tonight. Frowning, I imagined the card that Darren had left me. Could I explain about Gregor and trust the Knight of whatever? What if he knew exactly where Gregor was, or what to do about it? Besides, maybe I'd gain a little information about witches.

"Pho?" Tyler asked.

My stomach stirred, but I shook my head and lifted my heels off the polished wood floor. *Boots.* "I need to keep looking for Gregor."

CHAPTER 19

I slowed to a walk when I approached my apartment building. The taint of garbage and a hint of the distant lake drifted from the direction of the sun low on the horizon. The long shadows were comforting and familiar, reminding me of home. Darren's car was not parked across the road. Shailagh didn't wait by the oak. My new neighbor wasn't lugging crates. Flamingos watched me from the shadows.

Khimmer, wildlings?

None, Mistress.

I let out a deep breath and kept an eye out for Mrs. Forster. Tyler planned on picking up some Pho and leaving it in the fridge for later tonight or tomorrow. My growling stomach would have to wait while I fed Woo.

I had left Darren's sigil-marked card on the floor by my mattress. That call would happen before I ate. What would I do if he had Gregor's address? Threaten him? I'd never killed someone who wasn't interfering, part of my queen's assignments, or in immediate self-defense. That would be murder.

My heart felt heavy as I skipped up the stairs. Mrs.

Forster hadn't made it out by the time I was inside and apologizing to Woo.

The cinnamon scent surrounded me like a welcome robe. Woo whistled and climbed up the kitchen cabinets. "Miss me?" I smiled as I made two small piles for Woo of the cat treats and pistachios. The white stripes in their pink tail seemed to sharpen as they settled on the counter to eat. If I did have to leave, Woo could come with me. The thought dropped the grin from my face.

I stomped a couple steps for my bedroom and then grimaced thinking of my new neighbor. Phone out, I dropped my shorts to the floor. I needed a shower.

Darren's card had been shoved under the edge of the mattress. Call or text? I pulled up the phone, punched in the number, and put it on speaker as I stripped.

"Hello?" His voice had a nasal quality on the phone.

"Darren?" I ought to be sure before I started discussing symbionts and vampires over the phone.

I could imagine a smug grin from his tone. "Ahnjii Fate," he said my name slowly.

"Yeah. Listen, I've got a problem, other than Clarita." I took slow steps toward my bathroom. *Remove boots.*

Yes, Mistress.

The floor felt cold.

"Yes, Gregor Gehrke."

I shivered in the bathroom, staring at myself with wide, surprised eyes. "Yes. How did you know?" Anger flushed up my neck. When had he known? "You knew?"

"Since our last meeting." His voice remained calm, as if discussing reading a book. "I'm not surprised, considering your ability. You'll get more offers, I'm sure."

I didn't want any more, and wouldn't get them if I had to go into hiding. "What do I do?"

"You've already said no. Tell him no, or yes, as your interest dictates." Darren's tone remained nonchalant. "We've sent word to him about his latest threat. We could not abide such behavior, and he should know that. His family was included in the message, so there is no need to worry about his ultimatum."

A prickling chill rose up my neck. Darren knew where Gregor was. Did I need to know, or would the Knights take care of it? "Where is he?"

Darren laughed. "No. Let's have coffee. I'll tell you what I can. I'm surprised you haven't dealt with the Upre before this."

I didn't want Darren to question me any further and get suspicious about my origins, but I felt compelled to learn everything I could about Gregor. Meeting Darren in person was to my benefit because I couldn't truthsense over the phone.

"Tea," I said.

"Sorry?"

I began plucking my braid loose. "I prefer tea. I've got to shower. I'll meet you in your usual parking spot in half an hour."

CHAPTER 20

I stepped out the front door with the world in heavy shadows. I smelled floral from the shampoo. Music thudded from down the street. Darren's ratty car waited across the street, and I could make out the brim of his fedora. The breeze had gotten cooler, and I hadn't dressed any warmer than the black tank top and shorts I'd been wearing.

Khimmer, wildlings?

None, Mistress.

I had almost replied to Gregor, but resisted. My instinct told me that Gregor would not be cowed by the Knights, or anyone.

The Square Mug would not be open this late. I'd let Darren worry about the location. Maybe I could get my questions answered before we ended up someplace public.

The door to Darren's car groaned when I opened it, and the inside still had a light foul odor. We traded polite greetings while he twisted knobs and fought with the lever between us. We started onto the road heading through the apartments toward College Town.

"Where is Gregor?" I asked, knowing that he'd refuse.

He tilted his head as he pushed the lever to the side with a grinding noise and the engine pitch changed. "I told you that I wouldn't be divulging that information."

I waved into the air, mimicking a motion I'd seen Tyler make before. "I don't mean like his house address. Is he from America? Does he live in Florida?"

Darren hummed a single note before speaking. "Why do you want to know? Are you planning on taking his contract?"

I smiled, keeping my focus on the road. "It's certainly an option. Florida?"

"Not Florida."

I groaned. "Not helpful."

"You're not going to go kill him, are you?"

Turning to face him, I laughed. "You're the one who told me it's all taken care of. Should I worry that it isn't?"

We stopped at a corner while he hummed that same tone. Two girls on his side of the car studied us from where they leaned against a truck. The taller of the two had white or perhaps light gray hair. Straight and long, it stuck out against the growing shadows. She wasn't smiling.

"I should at least warn you that his enemies are usually removed with explosives. However, if you are considering his offer: Louisiana. Three families are there and twenty-nine Upre total."

My heart fluttered like a fish in the air. I'd just narrowed Tyler's search. Proud of myself, I relaxed in my seat with a grin. "Is Louisiana a nice place?" I might as well keep up the impression Darren had formed.

"Some parts are more tourist focused, like New Orleans, but most of it is rural and swampy." Darren ground his lever. "It's Mardi Gras. Ever been?"

Mardi Gras?

Unknown reference and little context, Mistress. Perhaps a date or holiday.

"Nope." I could answer it honestly, but still feared Darren's questions would place me outside of being from Earth. "You?"

"Not yet. I've been to New Orleans, but I don't get much time for parades or drinking, or any celebrations of that sort."

Very good, Mistress. It seems a local holiday.

I hadn't really cared, but wanted Darren on a topic where my ignorance about Earth didn't show. "Why not?" I asked, again, not caring. When we got to wherever he was going, I'd slip away and message Tyler. I couldn't say what I'd do if we found Gregor.

"Duty — to the Knights."

The statement made me draw a breath. There had been a time just a few months ago when my position among the Aegis monks as the Queen's First Assassin would have brought a similar answer. I had a Blessed Blade and thus a duty to the goddess Nyx and my queen. I faltered, flailing mentally to find some other question to keep him off my ignorance without showing it. "How long have you been with the Knights?" Hopefully Earth witches didn't already know the answer.

"Early; they approached my parents before I was in puberty." He didn't seem to mind answering, but there was a deeper purpose to his questions. As simple and focused on Darren as I tried to keep the questions, he wanted something. I could sense it.

We passed through College Town and headed toward the sun hidden mostly by the horizon. I squinted at the occasional beam that found the car. Dust covered the dash and the inside of Darren's windshield.

"When did your abilities first develop?" he asked.

I tensed, not wanting to get into this discussion. I still answered honestly. "Before I can remember. You?" The dread grew that he'd trick me into answering something that highlighted my ignorance of Earth.

"Same." He pulled into a plaza in front of shop that offered bubble tea.

I couldn't help but grin. How did he know what kind of tea I liked? "Looks good."

"They usually offer fries, or something fried, if you're hungry." He locked the lever into place.

My stomach growled. I had managed a quick bite of cold noodles, but wouldn't say no to fries. I had my harness released and stood outside the car before he opened his door.

He touched the hood as he passed. "You like Mustangs?"

Mustang?

A wild horse in context with the cowboy era, Mistress.

I peered at the menu as I stepped onto the sidewalk. Excited, despite my earlier dread. "Yeah, never ridden one though."

He paused, then jerked his thumb at his vehicle. "Not a car buff, huh?"

I glanced at the front and caught the raised filigree of a running horse. Earth people named their cars like animals and such. "Oh, sorry." I'd have to ask Tyler what type of animal a Prius was.

Darren stepped ahead to the door and grabbed the handle. He paused, searching my face. "We're still trying to determine where you came from."

I thought I staggered at the comment, but froze. The statement could have deeper connotations or it could be that they thought I was from a different country. I couldn't reply. Darren was a witch, and I had no idea how well he could determine lies.

When he shrugged and pulled open the door, my heart started beating again.

CHAPTER 21

INSIDE THE SHOP, I let Darren walk a couple steps ahead. My shoulders were tense as I replayed his question. Was he asking if I was from Earth?

Two couples talked and ate at tables while a busy dark-haired woman called out a greeting to us. The aroma of fried chicken overpowered any other scents. Metal banged in the back out of sight. On the counter, a pink boba tea sat beside a paper bag. My heels clicked on the shining floor.

Darren had said, "We're still trying to determine where you came from." He could mean what city or nation on Earth, or that the Knights thought I wasn't from this world. I took short breaths against a tight chest. I had an intention of engaging the topic, but wanted clarification. Laura's suggestion to leave popped into my mind with far less resistance than before.

"You should try the Love Potion," Darren said. He'd turned a step from the counter and faced me. If he saw the panic on my face, he didn't show it. "I like the Spiced Chai."

He didn't wait for my response as the counter woman asked for his order. "Spiced Chai milk tea and crispy tofu."

Darren turned to include me. "I bet she's going to want the fries."

I jerked into a reaction, ordering everything he'd suggested because I couldn't focus on their menu. The dark-haired girl smiled as she took my order, and I faked a response. Darren paid for everything.

What would the Knights do if they believed I wasn't from Earth? How did they know so much? Had I mentioned I wanted fries, or did they just watch me enough to know? Anger bubbled and I managed a deep breath. "Have you been here before?" While we waited for our order, we sat close to the door, away from the other patrons.

"No. When you said tea, I did a quick search." He idly scratched stubble along his jaw. "I wanted something with outside seating. Weather's good. Private."

"Your people seem well informed."

"That's our job." He glanced at the other couples. "Those good people have enough to worry about in this mess of a world. We keep a couple of disturbing elements off their plate."

Like me? I had a sense of danger from Darren which I hadn't felt before. Did they just keep people like Tyler from posting about the Fae or the others, or would they take things a step beyond that?

Wildling, Mistress.

I turned in my seat to look out the front window. *Where?* A car's rear lights darkened.

In that car, Mistress.

I saw a shape turn at the closed driver's window. Gray sky reflected off the glass. The sun had almost disappeared, leaving them a silhouette. The streetlights hadn't turned on yet.

Darren grunted. "I felt them, too." His chair scraped

across the floor as he stood. He strode out the door, holding his hat firmly on his head against the light breeze.

Cool air drifted around my legs and shoulders. I sensed he didn't want me to follow. The wildling had to be one of Clarita's pack. Surely they wouldn't work for Gregor.

Darren walked up to the car and motioned for the driver to roll down the window. A bearded man glanced toward me before answering. My anger bubbled up again, and my chair legs squeaked as I shifted to face him. They talked for a second, annoyance easily visible on the wildling's face.

The rear lights lit red as Darren waited. The wildling backed up and drove away too quickly for the small parking lot. What had been said?

"The fries are yours?" The woman's voice took a moment to register.

I spun and jumped up a bit too fast. My chair skidded, but didn't fall over. Feeling foolish, I laughed and headed for the counter.

She had light skin and dark brown eyes. Her smile and glances were inviting, but not intrusive. "I thought you were going to have someone join you." Her lips tightened slightly. "Maybe an ex?"

X?

From context, I would presume ex as in previous rela-tionship now ended, Mistress.

I scowled. "No. No. I don't have *any* relationship."

Her smile warmed. "Shame. My name's Kathy."

My head spun enough that I barely responded, glancing over my shoulder as I did so. "Ahnjii."

Darren still waited, as if watching the car leave.

"I like your choker." She touched her own throat, motioning with spread fingers.

I took a deep breath, offering her a more genuine smile. The thought of Gregor or Clarita causing havoc in this woman's life just because I took interest forced my expression to fade. I couldn't live like this. Kathy didn't need me in her life; no one did.

My mouth suddenly dry, I reached for my tea and straw. Her expression dropped, as I probably looked terrified. I was a mess.

A whiff of the fries left my stomach unsure whether to be hungry or sick. I still dreaded the Knight's question about my origin and hated Gregor and Clarita for making me hyper alert. My phone buzzed in my pocket, and my fingers paused in the air between straw and phone.

I chose the phone as Kathy busied herself wiping the counter.

I gasped when I read Deanna's message. Phone gripped in pale knuckles, I raced for the door and sprinted away from Darren as he called across the parking lot.

CHAPTER 22

FIVE FLASHING POLICE cars were parked in front of Deanna and Tyler's house. I gasped a ragged lungful of air as I slowed to a trot. Without the sun, garish blues and reds splashed on dark trees, beige walls, and the clusters of officers. It staggered my vision, snapping my attention from one colorfully lit panic to the next.

"TYLER HAS BEEN KIDNAPPED." Deanna had messaged me nothing more than those words. I should have warned Deanna during the arrest in Pensacola, or after. My chest felt heavy, and I found it difficult to take full breaths.

Gregor had done this, and I didn't have the energy to be angry. I was terrified. An officer waved me to a stop. In truth, I dreaded facing Deanna.

The night cool, I still had sweat under my arms. I flinched as a harsh electronic voice snapped over one of the police radios in an unintelligible squawk. The lights appeared to be the only activity as the officers talked to each other, except for the group of three who spoke with an emotional Deanna.

This was my fault. I'd feared that Gregor would

endanger my friends. Turben and the Aegis monks had been right all along.

I tapped at my bracelets nervously and shivered. Would I accept Gregor's contract now? Blood rushed up my cheeks, warming chilled skin. I would sign if that was my only way to free Tyler.

I wanted Shailagh's advice. She understood the Upre. Her magic could help. Staring at the surreal scene, I sent her the frozen emptiness inside. *Gregor took Tyler. Would Idin let her?*

Wildling, Mistress.

Rage exploded inside me. Fists clenched, I peered against the madness of lights. *Where?*

Driving past, Mistress.

A gray minivan trolled by the space left by the police cars in the street. I recognized the woman from the skirmish at the Lichgate tree, not from her face, but I sensed it was the one whose leg I'd stabbed. I sensed others with her, probably in the back behind tinted windows.

I glared, wanting to lash out against something that I could reach. Gregor hid in Louisiana, and Tyler would likely be there soon. As the minivan turned the corner, I checked my cell phone, expecting a message from the Upre, though I hadn't replied to his most recent text.

What if it had been Clarita who took Tyler? Perhaps she'd sent the minivan to collect me, but the police had scared them away. Somehow, I couldn't believe that this was something the wildlings would do. They seemed more direct. This had the smell of Gregor.

The officer who had stopped me was tall and athletic. She studied me, and likely had the entire time. There were neighbors in the yards watching, but only I had tried to intrude.

"I'm a friend of the family," I said.

The woman nodded, then spoke into a phone or something on her shoulder. It seemed an odd place to keep it. Deanna leaned in toward the officers, obviously distraught. One of the men asked her something, and she looked in my direction.

Deanna waved me in, one officer then the next gestured, and finally the uniformed woman me jerked her head toward them. "Be careful where you step."

"Yes." I couldn't tell why I responded, and only noticed I had after I'd started to pass her.

"There's no blood on the driveway," a man was saying to Deanna. "A takeout bag was dropped by the car. Witnesses confirm that this seemed quick, and the victim gave them no real struggle during the abduction. Could this be a fraternity prank?"

Deanna's tone bordered on hysterical. "This is no prank. Tyler does not hang out with that sort."

My arm muscles jumped under the skin at the officer's mention of blood, even the lack of it. What have I done? I'd find him. Shailagh might help, if she weren't prohibited. Even Darren might be an option, though I'd left him at the tea place.

Anger boiled up, and I clenched my teeth. I'd set a meeting with Gregor, play nice and subservient before I started peeling my way through his chest, until his symbiont decided it would be better to let me know where they held Tyler.

Deanna turned toward me, and her wide-eyed panic turned to a frown. "Ahnjii, what's wrong?"

I let my face relax and grabbed her in a hug. "When?" I asked. Shailagh might have some magic to help me track the kidnappers. I still shook, not from cold or panic anymore, but rage.

Deanna's voice broke as she spoke each sentence fired in rapid bursts. "An hour ago. Picked up dinner. I heard Tyler yell. Only reason I looked out. They chased Tyler to the front of the house." She ended in a dull whine that finished in a sob. "John's driving around, but he doesn't know what to look for." Her voice turned hard. "None of them do."

"Ma'am, what was your brother wearing?" a light-skinned man with a too bushy mustache asked. His studied me as we separated.

"Sibling," Deanna corrected. "Tyler had a black Arden Tee from Free People with thumb holes in the cuffs. I already described all this to the female officer. Black baggy short pants, I'm not sure of the brand."

He nodded, but didn't take any notes. Long hairs hung stiff over his lip despite the breeze. His eyes peered at my Nightarmor jewelry. "Ahnjii Fate." The officer made my name a statement. "And your relationship?"

"Close friend."

"Of course."

Lie. He didn't believe me. "We don't have sex. Tyler's not my lover. We are friends, as I am with Deanna."

He nodded again, in a way that had become irritating. "Where were you at the time Tyler Ramnath was taken?"

"You're wasting time," Deanna said. She pulled out her phone and began texting with flying fingers.

We were using time they should be looking for the kidnappers, but the police had been useless tracking John. I needed Shailagh to respond.

Khimmer, one hour ago? I still had a horrible sense of Earth time.

Feeding Woo, Mistress.

"I was taking a shower at my apartment."

"Was anyone with you?"

"In my shower?"

As one of the younger men chuckled, the bushy mustached man blustered and glowered. "At your apartment."

"Check in with Mrs. Forster, you'll enjoy talking with her. She's in the apartment next door." I gave them my address when they asked, and this he wrote down. After about three more useless questions, a siren sounded as an SUV raced down the street. Deanna broke away from us and headed toward it.

The officers questioning me paused, then jerked into a quick walk toward the vehicle.

An intense looking man with glasses jumped out of the driver's door and strode directly for Deanna. With an air of genuine concern, he gave her a quick hug. He didn't have on a uniform.

The man with the bushy mustache swore under his breath. I followed behind, and none of the other officers stopped me. They all had become alert and focused. This had to be their boss.

By the time we reached them, the new arrival had begun barking out orders. "I want equipment on the cells and landline in the house. The family is being set up to trace from New York if the ransom call goes there, which it likely will. Clear the street. Ms. Ramnath says there's plenty of room in the garage and gym to set up surveillance. We don't expect them back here, but they may do a pass or two, and I want each vehicle cataloged."

His face didn't show as much emotion as his eyes.

Locking on me through his glasses, he spoke to Deanna without turning. "Does she stay?"

"Ahnjii, yes. If she would." The latter comment was to me.

"Yes," I said, moving closer to Deanna.

"We'll need exclusion prints."

Khimmer?

Fingerprints, I surmise, Mistress.

I agreed and leaned against Deanna. During the papers to create my IDs they'd had me put ink on my fingers, a messy process. I would stay until Shailagh got back to me or Darren agreed to help. This man gave me some sense that they would do their best to find Tyler, but I doubted mentioning Gregor would do more than confuse the issue. Besides, the Upre seemed to have more connections than Tyler's family. I couldn't fight him on that level. Evidently Darren's Knights had as little power if they'd already sent him a warning.

For now, I'd support Deanna, but there had to be a better plan I could come up with. Shailagh was my best hope.

"What a horrible week," Deanna said as she leaned her head on my shoulder.

I couldn't bring myself to tell her it was my fault.

CHAPTER 23

DESPITE A TIGHT CHEST that had me wanting to pace about the room, I curled up on Tyler's bed with Jake and Willie. Outside the closed door the murmur of activity ranged about the house. Deanna spoke sharply at points. Noises came from every direction, and her two orange tabbies stayed in the bed with me, ears perked high and eyes wide.

The overwhelming sense of helplessness pressed down on me like a layer of dirt. The police were searching in the wrong places. "I don't like being stuck in here either," I said. They accepted my petting, but didn't purr. "It's better we stay out of the way."

One of the tabbies gave me an annoyed look. They were trying to listen to the commotion. I continued, "They're wasting their time expecting a ransom call."

I glanced at my phone, clear of any text from Gregor. The ransom was me. Shailagh needed to get back to me before he sent a message and I had to respond to him. The police were wasting their time.

"I've got three options," I told my companions. "I'm

ignoring any possibility that Clarita is involved and assume Gregor planned all this. First and worst, I confuse the police with a version of my conflict with Gregor that does not include Upre or my abilities. Second, I text Gregor, negotiate, and likely comply. Third, I hope that Shailagh will charge off to Louisiana with me and send him to Hades."

They both gave me harsh looks.

"Sorry, I'll be quiet." I ran my fingers through soft orange fur.

The room smelled of frankincense, a favorite scent of Tyler's, and I just sat doing nothing. Heavy wooden bookshelves lined three walls, with the only openings for doors and the window. The last wall had been painted a light purple, though monitors, desk, and the headboard hid much of it. An open energy drink sat under one of the dark monitors attached to the wall.

I jumped when Shailagh sent an image of the Lichgate tree. *Come.*

The glaring tabbies both stood.

"Sorry." I shoved my phone in my pocket as I stood. "Gotta go." The various conversations echoed from around the house as I stepped out of Tyler's room and carefully closed the kitties inside.

I sent Shailagh a confirmation that I would be there, but got no reply. Her initial contact had been short and absent of any emotion.

Deanna was talking in the kitchen with the intense man without a uniform before I burst in. "I've got to go check in with someone. Jake and Willie are locked in Tyler's room."

"Who?" the man asked.

"A friend." I waved him off and continued speaking to Deanna. "I'll be back as soon as I can. Please let me know if you find out anything."

She just nodded, but the man called after me as I ran for the door. The air was cold outside. The sun had abandoned us completely and left a of couple stars in the sky. The police cars were gone, and the streets quiet. The neighborhood acted as if my best friend had not been kidnapped.

I took off at a run. *Wildlings, Khimmer?*

No, Mistress.

I still hadn't forgotten about Clarita and grew more concerned as I approached the tree. Slowing my pace, I caught my breath as I jogged through the parking lot. The wildling's truck had been removed, and I couldn't see the marks of our scuffle in the darkness.

The light of a portal shone through the woods. Shailagh must have timed it so we'd arrive at the same time. I hoped she'd been healed. It had been a nasty wound.

The silhouette standing at the lit portal was not Shailagh.

My steps grew slower. *Who is it?*

The high Fae called Idin, Mistress.

I stepped closer. "Where's Shailagh?"

His voice had not gotten any friendlier since we last met. "The Council wants to ask you questions." He stood a step away from the tree and gestured toward the open portal.

Shailagh had warned me that the Council might be interested in Nightarmor. Was that what they wanted? I needed help from Shailagh, not more problems.

"I don't have time right now." I stopped, two steps away from him.

Idin scowled. "Make time."

"I'm sorry, I can't."

Nightarmor started to flow before I recognized the sound of a limb creaking. The branch slammed against my unprotected back. Like the wight's attacks, it carried a solid punch. Idin's aim was true, and I felt myself shoved into the portal.

The world tinkled like thin glass shattering. Light blinded me before I hit a slope of soft grass. Khimmer wrapped me in Nightarmor as I rolled to my knees.

Hades. The high Fae had tricked me. I jerked into a crouch, ready to fight.

The portal I'd been ambushed into shone bright and uncaring. The dark shadow of Idin grew inside. Had the high Fae known about Nightarmor? Did Shailagh tell them? I flushed at the idea of betrayal and being trapped.

A gray sky hung over me as Idin followed through the portal. An old tree, Lichgate had a massive trunk the width of Tyler's car that rose on a grassy mound the size of a house.

I spun around, but it seemed we were alone. I searched the forest around me, ready to call on weapons.

Idin had forced me to come here, but I saw no Council, not even another Fae. The rush of preparing for battle faded. After meeting Idin, I wondered how non-human the high Fae could be.

The woods were greener than I expected, with a dense wall of vines blocking any visibility ahead. Birds called from every direction in a chorus that enhanced the vitality of the trees. Even the feathery trees with their trunks deep in the water seemed healthy and vigorous. At my feet was a wet marsh that made me think of the wight, Theovole. My chest tightened at the memory.

I had no idea where we were. The portal had closed. "Don't do this," I said with a low growl. Frustrated and threatened, I felt my pulse rise.

Idin didn't speak as he approached. Examining Nightarmor, he had an appreciative look and an inquisitive tone. "What technology is this? Who are you really, Ahnjii Fate? Do you work for the government?" He shook his head. "No, that we would know." A scowl drew down his eyebrows, highlighting his stubby horns. "This complicates everything."

They hadn't known about Nightarmor until Khimmer had activated it. However, there had been danger. "Open the portal." I resisted calling for my sword.

"You'll talk with the Council first." His tone gruff, he pointed behind me.

The forest behind the portal tree did not look like Florida. "I'll just walk out of here then."

Idin sighed and rubbed the skin around one of his horns. Did they itch? "Don't."

Which way is Tallahassee?

Unsure, Mistress. East, that is left, based on the sun's position and present height on the horizon. I believe we would need to go south as well.

I took a step to go around Idin.

Vines rustled in the forest behind the portal to form thick mats of vegetation that hid the trunks. I could cut through it or climb over it.

I paused, stewing in anger and frustration. Tyler didn't have time for me to be stuck here with the high Fae. "Where's Shailagh?"

Idin snorted. "The Council has questions for you, that is all you should be concerned about."

I leaned close to him; Shailagh had always been uncomfortable with Nightarmor's proximity. "What if I don't want to answer their questions?"

He didn't flinch, but he coughed as he spoke. "They'll be persistent."

The temptation to start hacking my way out of the forest grew, but Tyler might be far from wherever Idin had taken me. Perhaps I could see Shailagh if I agreed. The high Fae might have answers about Gregor as well.

A small path of grass swerved behind me. I pointed. "Is that where we are going?"

Idin's cruel smile returned, reminding me yet again of the demons in Tyler's manga books. "Perceptive." He strode quickly through the grass, leaving me to follow.

There were dim orange shapes beyond the green.

Fae? I thought to Khimmer.

There are many ahead, Mistress.

I spotted sigils carved into trees, formed in vines, and woven from stems in bundles that dangled from branches. What would these tell another human? *Stay away? Go back?* I would probably be better off listening to their lies or warnings.

We were ten paces away when the verdant vines parted and created an arched opening perfectly aligned to the grass path that rose from the swamp. Roots formed two stairs just inside. Again, I was reminded of the dark horror that had been Theovole's cavern and took a tight breath. Little light shone inside, and nothing appeared to move. No one awaited us on the steps.

The Fae were spread in the trees above and ahead of us. I took a risk coming here; they could not compel me, but Shailagh had seemed sure they would be interested in Nightarmor.

I took the root steps slowly. The high Fae would learn from Idin about Nightarmor.

I stopped at the top of the stairs to let my eyes adjust to the dimness, believing that vines blocked light from the canopy above. Instead, the branches of trees had interwoven with their neighbors to form curving platforms and bridges. I could hear voices among the birds high in those shapes. The air smelled heady with life and scented with flowers.

I gestured overhead. "You live there?"

"None of your concern." Idin's eyes tightened, then he nodded. "Some of us."

Roots and limbs grew together to form a spiral staircase around a thick trunk to my left. Another wrapped about a wider tree deeper in the forest. Delicate flowering plants grew in clusters on the ground, dangled on the tree trunks, and blossomed heavily off the structures in the canopy.

Idin stomped deeper into the forest. I spotted a red-headed Fae on a distant bridge between two trees who had stopped to regard us. "Hurry," Idin said. "I'll not keep them waiting."

"Is Shailagh here?" I followed, my head swiveling to look for more Fae. If they all used their magic on me, I would have a long fight to get free.

"Liam's lips, spit that name off your tongue unless the Council asks for it." His voice was gruff.

I glared at the back of his head. My strides grew longer to keep up with him as we reached a darker section where the trees interwove thickly. A small group of orange shapes formed through the dark green. There were fewer high Fae in the canopy above. I'd become more annoyed than concerned. "I did not realize the high Fae would take people against their will. In fact, I'd come to believe you respected the rights of others." As I realized I sounded like Tyler, I scowled. "Or is that all you?"

"Witches should be more respectful."

"I wouldn't count on it."

The forest ahead had become black, partially from the falling sun. When Idin turned to glare at me, his eyes seemed to shine against the darkness. "You'll watch your tongue with the Council."

I couldn't help but enjoy the anger biting his voice. "That's not likely."

His anger felt palpable and the trees rustled, but he didn't drop a step. No branches attacked.

I faltered as we came to a stone arch, intricately carved with sigils. The forest grew up the side of a tall hill maintaining a dense cover so that the barest of light made it through. "What's in there?" I asked.

"The Council. Move it."

There was only blackness ahead. I had become curious about his Council. If I wanted to get back anytime soon, I probably needed to play along. They might even have information about Gregor. The only orange figures I could make down the corridor were straight ahead.

"Lead on, Grumpy."

CHAPTER 24

WE DREW CLOSER to the two high Fae, but they remained motionless until they each opened a massive door.

"Hades." I faltered a step at the size of the opening.

Dim light spilled out between stone slabs shaped to fit a pointed arch. As the doors became defined by light from the chamber within, I could not imagine a hinge that would support their weight, nor the strength that it took to move them. The guards wore shining armor that looked more like black porcelain than metal.

Stone steps rose at the edge of the opening, climbing into a dull yellow cavern that seemed to echo light with no source. Halfway up, ten steps or more, figures glowed through the carved stairs. They seemed to dangle ahead. I expected the musty smell of a cave, but the fragrance of gardens, earthy and sweet, hung in the air.

"Remove your helmet," Idin said, his voice hushed.

"Bite me." I grinned. I'd never gotten to use the phrase outside of joking with Vivianne. This seemed like a much better use. I didn't particularly trust the high Fae anyway. However, there were no trees underground.

His reply was not in English, but the tone indicated something unpleasant.

Translation?

Unknown, Mistress. No context.

The top of the cavern formed a dome where yellow swarming sparks trailed into view, almost reminding me of the wight's cavern. Any levity died inside me.

Another step brought a fringe of darkness where the flecks of light dove in and out. The inhabitants were distant orange shapes just past the top of the stairs. When we reached the top step, the high Fae hung deep in the fuzzy shadows that lined the back edge of dome.

Anyone other than the high Fae ahead?

It is dense stone around us, but I believe they are alone, Mistress.

Rippling water reflected the yellow lights, though not the orange figures. I did want to take my helmet off, just to see beyond Khimmer's vision. Idin gained a few steps ahead of me as he strode directly toward what seemed an underground river, albeit slow moving if at all. It stretched to the cavern's edge to my left and right.

Idin, perhaps annoyed at my attitude, ignored me. He stepped into the water, or more precisely, seemed to step on top of it. He was a quarter of the way across when I came to the edge and found stone risers just under the surface; around those oval shapes, the water looked black and bottomless.

Hades. I nearly lost my footing when the pedestal I stepped off dropped down with a light gurgling noise. No matter how fast or slow I paced, once I'd moved my boot off a stone, it disappeared. The sense of being trapped increased, and my pulse rose with it.

Focused on the water, I reached the far edge to find the

high Fae in a semi-circle. Idin waited for me, and nine orange shapes hung in the darkness. The yellow lights were far more prevalent than I'd first thought, many of them buried in the darkness and flicking out for just a second.

What is that? I peered at the fuzzy shadow that mounted tree height on the back wall.

I believe it is a type of moss, Mistress.

"There." Idin pointed to a pale circle in the stone floor.

I'd never seen moss grow that large, and considering the high Fae's magic, I didn't relish getting closer. Strolling as if confident toward the indicated spot, I studied one of the high Fae hanging above. They sat, as if on a chair or throne, cradled in the moss. Khimmer's vision and the distance above made it difficult to gauge definition, but I swore they had antlers. I had seen deer aplenty on Duruce, and the shape was familiar. Remembering the wight, those twisting spikes could have easily been branches growing out of their head.

Two paces wide, the light stone circle rested flush with the floor with a finger-widths gap around it. Sigils had been carved across its smooth surface. The surrounding gray stone appeared rough in comparison.

The yellow lights were closer but no more distinct. They ducked in an out of folds in the moss, defining the fringes of the plants with their passing. My apprehension calmed as I watched their dance.

"Ahnjii Fate." A woman above spoke with a stern authoritarian voice. "Is that your name?"

Which one is speaking? They were too high up for me to see distinct features.

The center one of the nine, Mistress.

Her question had a probing nature to it, reminding me of the questions that Bill asked. Did she have truthsense?

Shailagh had said many of the high Fae had a lesser form of it than my own. "You can call me Ahnjii." Tyler had given me the latter name as a joke and the reminder dropped a hole in my chest. *I've got to find them.* I clarified honestly to avoid the woman restating the question. "My name is Ahnjii."

I sensed a buzz and a male high Fae spoke the same strange language from my left. The woman replied quietly to him.

Translation?

I'll need more data, Mistress.

"Listen," I said. "Your thug dragged me here against my will. What do you want? I've got something important going on, and you're keeping me from it."

Shailagh might not be allowed to help, from the sounds of Idin's comments. Perhaps these high Fae would consider giving me some information, but at what cost?

"Remove your helmet."

Idin had seen Nightarmor form. Had he been able to communicate this, like Shailagh did with me? Either way, they would know eventually.

Be wary and ready to reform if they attack. Remove helmet.

Yes, Mistress.

Nightarmor flowed off my head to a murmur of comments that I hoped would help Khimmer's translations. Knowing someone's language when they didn't think you did could be very helpful. The woman who'd been addressing me argued a point with someone to her right.

They were all dressed in white robes from what I could see in the dim yellow light. The antlers or branches were dark shapes sprouting from elaborate white headdresses. Gems or glass glittered on their heads and clothing. The allure of the detail begged a closer look. I doubted they'd come anywhere near me or Nightarmor.

The woman regained order with a couple quick commands. A moment of silence descended, and the distant sound of dripping water echoed in the cavern. "Where are you from?" she asked.

My heart froze in my chest and blood pounded in my ears. "I came to Tallahassee from Slovenia."

She raised a hand when someone spoke in their language. Her eyes glinted from a yellow spark traveling between us. "Where are you from?"

I pushed down the panic rising in my throat. What would they do if they knew I wasn't from Earth? I didn't intend to highlight this question if I could avoid it.

I took a breath tried to gain some control of the situation. "What do you know of an Upre named Gregor Gehrke? He's kidnapped my friend in an attempt to force me to sign his contract."

The woman ignored my question and raised a hand at one of the others when they commented. A moment passed, allowing the trickling water to overcome the silence. She made an odd motion with her hand, flicking it sideways. "Where did you get this technology?"

I'd really hoped we'd avoided the discussion. Khimmer had been clear that both they and Nightarmor were a technology, though I found it hard to consider them that way. I had believed the gods had made them, and perhaps they had. "It chose me."

I felt the buzz, and more of the dangling figures spoke in their strange language. Khimmer would let me know if they could start translating. We'd done this before. Most recently when I learned English from Tyler, Deanna, and John.

Again, the woman raised her hand for silence before she

asked her next question. "Who do you work for? A government? A private organization?"

My duty to the Queen could not be considered active, with me here on Earth. "At the moment, I work for a lawyer named Bill, no government or company."

The buzzing felt almost audible. The high Fae burst into discussion, ignoring me. The air was cool on my face, while inside Nightarmor I stayed warm. I could smell the moss tinged with a flowery note.

"Confirm you do not work for the United States government or any of its agencies." She had to be using truthsense, or something very close.

"Nope, I do not."

She worked through a list of governments, some of which I'd never heard of, and even some companies with strange names. Bored, I would have checked my phone for messages, but didn't want to remove Nightarmor. The device would have buzzed and vibrated if Gregor had sent a message.

Her last question caught my attention. "Do you work for the group presently known as the Knights of the Ascendant Concors?"

I raised my eyebrows. Obviously they would know of each other. "No. However, they attempted to stop Gregor." At least, Darren had said they had, and he'd spoken the truth. What did I really know about them?

Frustration bubbled in my chest, and my tone carried it as I raised my voice. "Are you going to help me? If not, let me out of here. I need to find my friend. I can't do that standing in your dank cave."

I'd foolishly followed Idin across that water, and had no idea how deep it was or if I could cross it. Beyond that, I'd still have to hack my way through the vines, and if they didn't want to let me go, then I imagined the high Fae would keep raising obstacles.

I believe you should raise your helmet, Mistress. It is possible one of the others has suggested that you be disposed of.

Anger boiled, and my cheeks flushed. Everyone who knew the high Fae had warned me about them. Even Shailagh hadn't trusted the Council with news of Nightarmor. I'd been foolish to come this far. They weren't going to help me.

The woman began quieting the others.

Be ready, I thought to Khimmer.

Yes, Mistress.

She studied me from her perch. "You will not tell us where you come from?"

I answered her question by ignoring it. "When you tricked me into coming here, I was working with Darren of the Knights to resolve my issue with Gregor." I spoke truly, but hoped that they would believe he knew where I had run off to. I could have told him. "If you will not help me, then I will be leaving, as he is awaiting my return." I hoped they would consider that Darren might know of our meeting, and that there could be some consequences attached to that. As in Gregor's world of power, politics, and deception, I was out of place in these sorts of circumstances. Blade, armor, and someone to kill were the rules I understood.

They erupted into debate, and I waited for Khimmer. A flicker of urgency swelled inside, but I couldn't find Tyler without more information or in response to Gregor contacting me. I didn't like the latter option.

My translation is flawed, but six of the Council believe you are a threat, Mistress. The title of the woman asking the questions is Leric, of this I am sure. She credits you with being a resource, if handled properly. Her argument has persuaded four besides herself not to attempt to kill you, but they vary in their next course of action. There are repeated terms that have unreliable context.

I glanced back at Idin; he hadn't moved any closer and bore no weapon. The water, stone doors, and a small town of high Fae with trees sat between me and the woods outside. I had to gain their trust. Politics didn't suit me.

I smiled amiably as the conversation stopped.

The woman, the Leric, rose from her seat. The moss undulated, and her body glided down and toward me without swaying or taking a step. Her robe looked like fur and silk, as fine as any that Queen Mehlia had ever worn. Red and blue jewels adorned her neck and ears. Clear diamonds or glass glittered on her clothing and headdress. Antlers sprung from her head close to where Idin's nubs grew. Stiff cloth formed the headdress, and dusty white horns joined at the forehead and swept to the back in points. Her ear tips poked through amid sweeps, folds, and sparkles. Pale orange hair rolled across her shoulders. She did not return my smile. Sandaled feet remained on a carpet of moss. "Few witches respect us anymore, but most have a healthy fear. You do not."

I shrugged, pauldrons grating. "I've met worse, Gregor being on the top of my list at the moment. I do respect the high Fae and all your abilities; I consider Shailagh a friend," I said honestly.

She frowned, but let me continue.

"Trust is lacking in our relationship at the moment, on both sides. I'm quick to trust, some say too quick. Idin's trick has made me suspicious and cautious, but even considering that, I would not betray your trust to anyone you do not wish to know about you. I keep my promises, which is why some of your questions will go unanswered. No one has sent me to find information about your people. I came solely to seek Shailagh's help, and would accept yours."

I finished, hoping at least not to have to fight my way out of the cave. The buzzing started again almost to the point of hiding the distant trickling of water in the background. If I were lucky and came out of this with some information on Gregor, this would have all been worth it.

"You are willing to incur this debt?" the Leric asked me.

"Debt?"

She blinked as her eyebrows raised. "You would ask a favor of the high Fae Council." She spoke it as a statement. Evidently any favor was expected to be returned.

"Yes, of course. Within the parameters of our existing discussion. I won't answer questions that risk betraying other confidences or the ones I haven't answered today, unless we become closer friends and I choose to." I forced myself not to squirm. Wording the answer to this woman was as bad as asking a question of Shailagh.

"Acceptable. We only know that Gregor Gehrke resides in New Orleans. The Knights should have his exact address, as they track those sorts of things. The Upre are despicable and we have no dealings with them." Her eyes tightened. "When your situation is resolved I will . . . ask that you return here so that we may talk further. Perhaps then we will discuss your debt, or perhaps not."

The buzzing intensified, but I ignored it. "Thank you." I had hoped for more, but the city would have to do. That and not slashing my way out. Playing nice had worked. "I like the . . . uh . . ." I said, circling my fingers around my own head. "Very sparkly and pretty."

She didn't smile. "You may leave now."

I jumped when the rolling carpet of moss began to lift

her away. After a moment, I turned toward Idin and thought his teeth might break, he scowled so hard. I smiled despite his glare. I still had to decide if I would head to New Orleans on my own, try to turn Deanna's police in that direction, or bring it to Darren and threaten to go wreak havoc in the city unless he brought me.

I motioned to the water. "After you, Grumpy."

CHAPTER 25

I FOLLOWED Idin into the forest outside the stone arch, barely able to see since the sun had disappeared. If the high Fae used lighting, I saw no glimmer of it. Crickets and frogs had replaced all but the occasional bird. Cool air brought fresh scents.

"Where is this place?" I asked my fourth question since we'd left the Council, and still he didn't answer. Idin didn't appear to like me.

Carpets of stars peeked through the canopy above, and I guessed we were closer to the edge of their town, or whatever they called their forest home.

Other than Shailagh's boss, what role did Idin play with the Council? He'd kept quiet throughout the proceedings. One of my first unanswered questions had been about Shailagh. She might be in the trees above.

Had she betrayed me directly or had she been tricked as well? Even the question hurt. Still, I reached out through her magical earring. *Leaving now.* I visualized the canopy above. If she were a friend, she might worry that I would not escape the Council.

There was no immediate response, but I noticed a strange sensation that I had never considered before. There was the faintest buzzing that told me the message had been sent. If it weren't for the buzzing that had occurred in the caverns, I wouldn't have given it any thought. They had been using something similar to communicate.

Khimmer, did you sense a buzzing in my mind just now?

Buzzing, Mistress? I did not.

I would pay more attention next time. A grin crept onto my face at the thought of eavesdropping on the Council on top of Khimmer's translation.

Birds called out as we exited into the swamp before the portal tree. Stars lit the sky and pools of water. Off to my right, something small splashed.

When Idin reached the tree ahead of me, the roots began to glow, and a bright portal climbed up and split the trunk. Shailagh hadn't responded. I paused, giving him a chance to lead the way.

He waved me on with a gruff voice. "Go."

I supposed there was no reason for him to go, just to come right back. My right foot stepping into the light, I turned with a smile and one last question. I pointed to my own forehead. "How long do those take to grow out?" Motioning upward, I indicated antlers.

He grumbled in his language and pointed into the portal.

Translation?

I could be wrong, Mistress, but I believe he called you a dribbling, onion-eyed, canker-blossom.

The tinkling of the portal danced in my ears. I emerged in the darkness of the park around the Lichgate tree laughing at Idin's curse.

Nightarmor poured up my face, stifling my outburst.

A muted gunshot rang out and a bullet hit me square in the chest, burning a hot blister through my tank top. One orange shape stood four or five paces ahead of me, and a second grew redder, moving through the brush to my right.

Dory.

I stepped into a second bullet while I pulled the spear from my back with one hand. The burn felt like a hot coal inside the armor.

Run, Mistress! The caliber is too high. Khimmer sounded frantic.

Dashing two steps toward the gun, I spun with my swing so that the tip overshot the wildling and the trajectory turned to the side of its neck. Through Khimmer's vision I could make out the changing face of a wildling. Eyebrows were growing more pronounced, and the jaw widened, protruding slightly to accommodate their teeth. A third bullet fired, but I felt no impact. I wouldn't slice flesh, but the shaft cracked into them hard enough I feared I might have broken bones.

Before the first wildling fell, I crouched, gained two hands on the shaft, and slipped it up and into the stomach of the oncoming attacker. Already shifted, this one might have had some feminine features, though the heavy jaw made it difficult to discern. Its arms had lengthened, and claws scraped against my gauntlets.

I recognized the distorted human face. Clarita had turned dark orange-red in Khimmer's vision. Shreds of clothing hung at her waist and shoulders. She'd been waiting for me.

As I spun to the side, tossing her to the ground, she raked my helmet with screeching claws. The impact slapped me to the side and would have torn my head off without Nightarmor.

I rose to a ready stance, spear tip pointed to her throat. My pulse pounded, not just in the excitement of battle, but in anger. I hesitated, not willing to kill her. My chest burned from the gunshots of the other wildling, who had fallen and not moved. I may have already killed another wildling.

She knocked aside my spear with a growl and leaped to her feet. Her strength was brute force and the ability to take painful blows. I had training, armor, and weapons.

Anyone else would have seen the death I promised, but she fought anyway.

I flipped the spear to my back and Nightarmor absorbed it. My first reaction was to stab and kill.

"Going to rip your head off." Clarita's voice sounded like gravel lodged in her throat.

She leaped at me with arms outstretched. I let her grab Nightarmor's helmet as I absorbed her initial momentum and rocked on both heels. Her grip was fierce, though Nightarmor would not twist.

I shifted a leg behind me to position her weight toward my back before I leaned forward. Turben had often used a similar maneuver on me. Clarita's feet scraped against Nightarmor's boots as I lifted her.

Rolling one shoulder, I flipped her onto her back. Long dark nails screeched on metal. I threw my left elbow back and slammed into her ribs. The aim had been low enough not to shatter the bone into lung. I heard the telltale snap and it reverberated in my armor. Clarita gasped, so I knew she felt some measure of pain.

Spinning away and to my feet, I stomped a heel into her opposite side to break another of her lower ribs. She squeaked, likely barely able to take a breath. One of the newer Aegis monk trainees had broken my rib once. The pain had been debilitating. I counted on that.

Her arm barely offered resistance when I grabbed her wrist, and she only reacted when I caught the elbow with my other hand. I twisted and thought the overly long limb would shatter before she rolled onto her face. She only needed to stay alive. I needed to be done with this and tracking Gregor.

Still holding the arm, I dropped one knee to her spine, knowing the pressure it put on her ribs. "This has to end." I needed to find Tyler, not play with wildlings.

She measured out words in short breaths. "The others will be here soon."

"And what will they think when they find you beaten and subdued?" I hated the pain I was putting her through, but I needed it to be over.

"They will still hunt you."

"Then we both lose." I needed something more to offer her. "You more than me."

Her voice still sounded like grating stone, but it diminished. "I've already lost them." She spoke the truth. Whatever internal politics had played out, I was her last ploy to keep her position.

I'd just negotiated with a high Fae Council Leric, whatever position that was. "What if you've beaten me but allow me to live, with the promise of a debt owed to you and your clan?"

She took a moment. "I would never agree to that. You certainly wouldn't."

What more could I give her and her clan to raise her status? If they took down Clarita, would they give up this vendetta? "I have other abilities. Witches' abilities. I can truthsense. I know any lie I hear."

"Truly?" she asked.

I laughed. "Yes."

CHAPTER 26

I sat against the base of the Lichgate tree, trying to look defeated. No police had arrived to investigate the gunshots, which surprised me. Clarita had assured me that she knew another wooded area behind us if the authorities interrupted us. Despite the cold air, I smelled like sweat and what I swore was burnt flesh. The wildling I'd knocked unconscious had risen and stood a few paces away as my unstable guard. Clarita had returned to her human form and stood stiffly addressing the three wildlings who arrived.

Khimmer, other than these five, am I missing any?

None, Mistress.

I didn't care what the pack thought of my supposed surrender, if it would end this. Shailagh still hadn't responded to me, and the sense of betrayal from her only grew. Idin and the high Fae were behind me for the present, though I'd honor the debt to both them and Clarita.

Gregor was in New Orleans. I could imagine no way to convince the police to look for him there. If I suggested it, the impossible explanations I would have would just tie me in Tallahassee.

I would go to New Orleans, but if it were as large as Tallahassee I'd have little chance of finding Gregor or Tyler. Neither Vivianne nor Laura would get near human technology, so their internet search abilities were worse than my own.

I needed to call Darren.

Clarita beckoned, and as I rose a blister on my chest burst. I felt the dampness on my tank top. I'd need a quick shower and a change of clothes before meeting with Darren. I hoped he didn't go to bed early.

"This witch," Clarita said, pushing me slightly in front of her, "owes me a debt now, owes us a debt, which we will take at a time of our choosing. She has the full measure of a witch's empath ability and can sense truth from lie. Equally, her prowess in battle is unmeasured against all but my own. I alone know her weakness, and she will not risk defeat at my hands."

It wasn't exactly the wording I'd suggested, but the male she'd been concerned about, a tall man in his human form, did not challenge her. Clarita had been clear that his dissension would be disastrous for us both.

Clarita continued with a braggadocio tone. "The high Fae, Shailagh, will account for her part as well. The next time we learn of her presence in Orlando, I will hunt her down and she too will pay her due."

The other wildlings glanced at each other with a few malicious grins. I'd pass that warning along the next time I spoke with Shailagh. The scent of their stale sweat had begun to taint the cool air. Having them off my trail was worth listening to Clarita's oration, but I did have other matters to get back to.

I'd learned a couple interesting things about wildlings in our skirmish, which Clarita had expected me to know. First, they healed much of their wounds by changing from one form to the other. She still walked a little stiffly, so there had to be limitations. Second, they used a lot of energy shifting and needed rest and food afterward.

I did have to wonder how they would be getting back to Orlando. They were mostly nude in their human form. They could drive, I'd learned, so they likely had vehicles and spare clothes.

They left me at the Lichgate tree after Clarita delivered a few grandiose warnings. I watched their human shapes jog into the brush.

Alone? I thought to Khimmer.

Yes, Mistress.

Remove armor.

The air proved cooler than I'd guessed.

Hoodie.

Nightarmor poured over my torso, arms, and head with a looser, pliable metal. Fatigue hung heavier than the clothing. I stumbled toward the parking lot and the roadside, digging into my pocket for my phone. Gregor had not messaged me yet. Why not?

How long would it take to drive to New Orleans?

I don't have an exact reference, Mistress. Five or six hours would be my best estimate.

Shuffling across the dirt, I texted Darren, "You still up?"

"I am. Would you care to explain why you left in such a hurry?"

"Pick me up at my place in an hour and we'll talk about it." Would I mention the high Fae? Might as well, it seemed they all knew each other. "About New Orleans?"

Darren didn't reply immediately. Wind blew down the

road, and the lights seemed far apart. A car sped toward me. I alternated checking between my phone and the headlights between each slow step. It rumbled past with a thick plume of noxious exhaust.

"ONE HOUR," Darren replied.

I checked the time before shoving my phone back in my pocket. It showed 10:12 p.m. Breaking the day into twenty-four segments seemed arbitrary to me, but Tyler had explained it once.

More than a little tired, the walk home took longer than usual, and I apologized to Woo when I went straight for the tea kettle. "Gregor took Tyler, Woo."

They whistled as they scrambled up to the counter.

"I'll boil enough water for noodles too." I pulled up my shirt. One blister marked the inside of my left breast. The second was below it at the bottom of my ribs.

I'd been brutal with Clarita, but it had worked. That level of viciousness always plagued me more than a clean kill. I sidled up to the counter for a hug. Woo obliged, nuzzling my neck. "How was your day?"

If the sun were up and Laura had been at her studio, I would have called her. She'd been right to warn me about the high Fae all along. I'd love to talk things through with her. Not to mention, she would also heal the blisters.

I ate some of the noodles with Woo, drank a cup of tea, and steeped a second before jumping into the shower. Sticky cartoon bandages applied to my blisters kept an ointment Tyler had bought from smearing. So many things reminded me of them.

Dressed in the same shorts with fresh underwear and a clean tank top, I drank my last cup of tea looking out at Darren's car parked across the street. He was early. I intended him to give me Gregor's address. The high Fae had seemed sure that the Knights would know. Woo clung on my belly, probably sensing I was leaving again. They had camouflaged when I'd slid the sheet aside to peer out. I scratched black fur that matched my top. If Darren looked up, he'd think I had an itch.

"I'm going to go look for Tyler," I said to Woo. "If I head to New Orleans, expect Laura to come feed you."

Woo nuzzled and let out a sad whistle.

When I walked through the pink birds, Darren watched me through an open window. His expression showed a hint of annoyance. He spoke as I crossed the street. "That's all you're bringing with you?"

I paused. "Bringing with me? Where?" I'd assumed we'd get tea at one of the late night restaurants. They usually had a bland tea of some sorts.

"New Orleans." He started up his car and spoke above the rumbling engine. "That's where Gregor Gehrke is, and as I've just figured out, where you assume your kidnapped friend has been taken. Is that why you ran?"

The headlights lit the dangling branches, brush, and grass ahead. Fumes reeked despite the brisk breeze. A dark satchel lay on the back seat nearly the same size as my flowery one. Darren was going to help me find Tyler. My chest filled with tight hope.

"Yes." I took a step, answering him, but wanting to run to the passenger side before he changed his mind. I spoke quickly. "Deanna had messaged me about Tyler. I should have explained before I ran out of there." My lips flickered a chagrined smile for the weak apology. "I know it was Gregor."

Darren adjusted his straw fedora with two fingers. "Could be your wildling friends."

I shook my head and ran around the front of his car.

The door screeched as I wrenched it open. "No, I just worked out things with them. That's all good. I texted you immediately after." I fumbled for the harness, then remembered to close the door. Through his open window, exhaust blended with the stale reek of his car.

He raised his eyebrows, but made no move to wrestle the lever in the floor that would make us move. "You worked out the vendetta with a wildling pack?"

I bobbed my head in a cross between a nod and shrug, then tapped the black knob at the top of the lever. "Yes, I owe Clarita a favor — a debt."

Darren's eyes widened. "Do you think that's wise? What if they want you to kill someone or commit some other crime?" He still didn't move for the little black ball or any of the pedals.

Frustration gurgled up in my throat. "I told her no stuff like that. Can we go?"

He shook his head in a way that told me he disapproved, but pressed pedals down, and something made a grinding noise when he moved the lever. "You might come to regret this obligation."

I tapped one of my armbands. We were going to directly confront Gregor. It would take hours. "I'll probably have more trouble with the debt I owe the high Fae Council lady now."

We had just started past the cars parked outside the student housing when Darren swerved, nearly hitting two young women walking along the road. They swore and made the gesture Tyler loved so much. "The high Fae?" His voice pitched higher than normal. "What? When? The Council itself?"

The two girls were still swearing behind us. "I thought I

was meeting Shailagh." My lips tightened at her name. "Would she betray me?"

Darren cranked his window up. "Yes. High Fae cannot be trusted. Why would you allow yourself to become indebted?" He snorted and his tone became sharp. "Who raised you?"

The last comment sounded less than an actual question and more like an insult. I ignored it. "Well, I'm in their debt, but within certain agreements. I wouldn't have had to barter for Gregor's location if you'd told me." It wasn't exactly true. I'd partly been trying to get out of there.

We turned a corner, and Darren ground the lever into the floor of the car. "I should have contacted you immediately. I was miffed. Has Gregor contacted you?"

"No, but obviously your warning didn't matter to him."

"If he kidnapped your friend."

"He did." I drew a deep breath to calm myself. "What are we going to do?"

"Flemming is on his way there now to deal with Gregor."

"To free Tyler?"

"If Tyler is there, then that is the intent." As we sat at a red light, Darren pointed to a convenience store and raised his eyes questioningly.

I shook my head at his offer; we had to hurry. "What are you doing with me if Flemming is going to New Orleans?"

"I'm assigned to you."

They were worried I would attack the Upre, and I would. "To protect Gregor."

Darren pulled into the convenience store parking lot, despite my prior refusal. "Yes. I gather you would have gone to New Orleans, with or without me?"

I frowned as he parked. This trip might leave me stuck

on the outside of the situation. Did it matter if Tyler were freed? "I would have found a way to get to New Orleans."

He parked, turned off the lights and engine, and studied me. "This is partially for your benefit. Extortion or kidnapping in order to compel agreement to a contract is prohibited. All Upre know that. If Gregor has kidnapped Tyler in order to persuade you to sign, then the Knights are within their rights to become involved. However, you would not be protected if any — if you caused any accidents to occur."

"Protected?" I asked. If Tyler were free, I'd take my chances.

"Much like wildlings, Upre can be defensive and vengeful of their own. They rely on their relationship with the Knights and would not see it strained. Your situation with them would be different." Darren's door creaked as he opened it. "Chips, bottled water? Do you like cold tea? It's gonna be five and a half hours to get there."

I growled and shoved my door open. Darren led the way inside, and I stomped down aisles, randomly grabbing snacks. We shouldn't be wasting time, but it wouldn't matter if the other Knight, Flemming, would be negotiating. I should be grateful. My best solution was to hack open Gregor to get at the symbiont. The Knights seemed more adept at this world of power and politics. If they freed Tyler and kept Gregor at bay, what did I care?

The Knights were keeping me out of trouble, restraining me. After all that had gone on for the past couple days, I didn't want to be held back.

When I started to pay, Darren waved me aside and used his own card. As the man at the counter bagged our supplies, Darren tapped the card on the counter. "Metal."

I didn't ask what he meant. It was going to be a long ride.

As we stepped into the chill air, Darren explained. "Gregor's people are pushing for metal credit cards, just to hassle the high Fae. Petty, right?"

I glared. "You're not in any hurry because you just need to keep me away from Gregor while Flemming deals with him."

Across the car's roof, Darren glanced at me from under the brim of his hat. "We'll be there when it matters."

Damn me to Hades. The Upre and the wildlings weren't the only ones who wanted vengeance.

CHAPTER 27

WE DAWDLED the entire trip to New Orleans, but somewhere along the way Darren became concerned. His occasional texting grew more frequent as we stopped countless times for three or four gallons of gas. I sensed the worry, but he wouldn't respond to my questions.

We took a long bridge across flat water that Darren promised led directly to the city where there were flickers of lights ahead. The sun still had not returned. "Hades. Are you going to tell me what's wrong?"

A massive truck passed on our left and added to my anxiety along the strip of man-made stone stretching across the water toward distant lights. Darren's car stunk of the wet peanuts he'd been buying. The tires smacked at regular cracks in the road. He didn't answer.

"The world is shifting. Strange things are happening. We've got trouble in eastern Europe we haven't had since the middle ages. Not Upre."

I doubted this had anything to do with his unease, but perhaps a random answer to my earlier question. It was conversation if nothing else.

"What do you think is causing it?"

"Started about the time you began stirring up problems." His focus remained on the road ahead, but I swore he wanted my reaction.

I laughed. He couldn't possibly blame everything on me. "Why don't you tell me what's going on with all these messages you send every time we get gas? I doubt it has anything to do with me or any place outside of New Orleans."

He let out a long sigh. "Flemming is off the radar. He went to Gregor's estate three hours ago, just after midnight. His phone signal is gone, among other things. We've got others on their way, but I'm the closest now, and I've got you to worry about."

I stiffened at the last comment, but it was valid. "What's the plan?"

Darren cleared his throat. "How about I drop you off at an all-night diner and scope out the situation?"

"What if you have the same problem Flemming did? You could use someone if things get difficult." I tried not to let my anger seep into my tone. The Knights were dancing around this whole situation and Gregor had still not contacted me. I knew my emotions were involved. Tyler had been gone overnight, and I couldn't know their treatment.

Darren's usually casual demeanor changed as his eyes hardened and his tone flattened. "Flemming walked in, not expecting an issue. There shouldn't have been a problem. Our understanding with the Upre leans heavily in our favor. If non-witches found out about them, they'd be eradicated." He adjusted his hat. "I'll be doing recon, not engagement."

"Meaning Tyler rots wherever Gregor has him stashed."

"I don't think your friend is in any immediate risk."

"You didn't think Flemming was either."

Darren tilted his head without a response. I took it as an agreement to my point. Everything he'd said was true, or he believed it to be so. I glared at the glass.

The glow of the city hung flat on the horizon with a few pinpricks of lights. The tallest, perhaps closest, structure had a blinking white light. Another massive truck passed, and I sipped on cold, stale tea, searching for a way to convince Darren to allow me to be involved. I had come too far to sit idly in some restaurant.

"If you're not going to try and get Tyler out, what do you intend to do?" I asked.

"I'll gather information so we can formulate a plan. Two other Knights will be arriving this afternoon and evening. We'll approach Gregor in a group, aggressively if necessary." Darren's crisp tone changed with a harsh note. "This Upre is possibly a greater danger to more than just you and your friend. Containment is paramount. I will not risk bringing your unpredictable behavior anywhere near him. If need be, we will both sit at the diner and let the other Knights handle this."

I threw my hands up, not caring that I spilled tea on his floor. "How can you expect me to just sit there and hope that Tyler survives?"

"If you let me go ahead, then we might have better success at protecting your friend when we face Gregor. Your resistance will only add risk to the situation."

I slammed my drink into the cup holder and ran my fingers through my hair, clasping the base of my braid with both hands. Darren was unmovable. If we both sat at the diner, him guarding me, then I *would* be risking Tyler. *Hades.* I had no choice.

"Fine." I spit the word out.

A darker mass lay ahead as the bridge neared land. I had expected buildings, but it looked more like trees. My jaw hurt from clenching it. After a minute of silence we reached land, and thin trees dotted the sides of the road. Streetlights lit the highway ahead. The only sign I had of New Orleans was the glow on the horizon.

Darren's voice resumed his conversational tone. "It's Mardi Gras. Going to be busy." We sped past an exit, and still there were no buildings.

I didn't care about their holidays and refused to engage him. It took a few more minutes of silence before we reached some residential houses with palm trees that someone had planted. The buildings grew as we drove, until it looked like some parts of Tallahassee. When Darren pulled off an exit, my pulse sped, even though I knew I was to be dropped off.

We pulled into a gas station, and he had me pump another two noxious gallons into his car while he went inside. Businesses and short homes were scattered around us, and the air had a cold bite to it. I glared at the few cars rumbling along the road and wondered where a person like Gregor would live. It would be someplace fancier than this. The sky had turned gray on one edge, promising that the sun would return.

I stalked back to my seat and wished I had one of the long-sleeve shirts Doris had bought me. I had no intention of letting Darren know about Nightarmor. It had probably been the reason some of the high Fae had wanted me dead. The Knights didn't seem that much more friendly.

Darren had mapped a location on his phone and drove through city neighborhoods that could have been Tallahassee. Nothing looked like a rich person's neighborhood. The deeper we got, the slower we traveled, and the sky got lighter.

"Mardi Gras," Darren said, trying again to engage me. "They'll close up the roads for parades west and southwest of here."

"Will I be waiting all day?" I asked with as sharp a tone as I could. "At this diner? Won't I be suspicious?"

We turned onto a tight one-way street with parked cars that made it even narrower. The houses looked different, many with porches on the second floor.

"Wander about if you choose. I'll call when I have news."

He hadn't answered whether I'd be waiting all day. The windows looked ornate, but not in an affluent way; they were too old. I would have enjoyed visiting, on any other occasion. People walked leisurely and with purpose down the sidewalks. We passed a three-story building with railings at each floor. I peered around when Darren stopped.

"I'll call you in a bit. Just give me some time to look around." He pointed to a white building with a second-floor porch.

The smallest pink car I'd ever seen was parked in front of it. Lights shone through the windows of two dark green doors. An older man with a flat hat walked a black and white dog.

"Here?" I unbuckled my harness and a car beeped behind us. "You'll call me?"

"Yes." Darren tilted his hat back and gave me a very sincere look. "Soon."

His car door squealed as I stepped out. Darren drove off when I closed it, and the driver behind glared until I crossed the street. I thought he might hit my heels. Tired, my body felt heavy and adrift at the same time. The sign on the door offered eggs. I wasn't hungry. Salt air drifted amid all the other scents of the city.

I wandered, following the old man and his dog until they stopped to sniff flowers. The people appeared pleasant enough, though I received odd looks, probably because I was freezing. If I could find a secluded place, I could have Nightarmor form a hoodie.

The sun had risen when I turned a corner, felt the hairs go up on my neck, and looked up to a second-floor balcony two buildings down.

An older woman with a steaming mug leaned on the railing, watching me. Her hair swept from her right ear up and over her head, short so it hung just over her left ear. It was shaved slightly on the right side and all white, then dyed blue at the top and deep purple on the left. Simple earrings dotted both of her lobes. Her eyebrows were a reddish-brown and curved over hard, dark eyes. She neither smiled nor frowned.

I shuffled on the sidewalk on the opposite side of the street, and we kept looking at each other.

Wildlings? Upre? I thought to Khimmer.

Nothing, Mistress.

I let out a breath I hadn't realized I was holding.

The woman had tattoos on her neck and the hands holding the cup that she did not drink. Her skin sagged with age that didn't touch her eyes. She wore a brown dress and a pale green shawl. A crawling vine blossomed with yellow flowers on the rail where she rested.

When I reached the point opposite her with my neck craned, she straightened, and gestured for me to wait as she took her cup inside.

I paused, peering at her head as she disappeared inside. Why should I wait? There was little else I needed to be doing, and the strange interaction we'd had made me curious. I shivered in the chill breeze and waited.

A MAN SLOWED as he passed, eyes on my chest, and I folded my arms while I waited for the woman. Pairs of people on the street talked as if the rising sun had rung the morning bell.

"Hades." I swore at the biting breeze as it took the corner. It stirred leaves on the few green vines that trailed metal rails and whipped around me.

Her hair bright, the old woman appeared at a gate to the stairs in the opposite building. I expected some squeak from the black and rust hinges, but she stepped through silently, eyes focused on mine. She held a bundle of black cloth in her hands.

The traffic on the narrow street was quiet, but she crossed as if it didn't exist.

"You're not from here." She shoved the black bundle at me. "And not particularly bright if you're walking about in that getup."

"I'm visiting." I opened up a thick black shawl and stared at it.

"It goes on your shoulders. Who are you visiting?" She

had a coiled green snake tattooed around her neck. "Don't bother answering with another lie. Now I'm curious. Why are you in New Orleans?"

I swallowed and slid the warm knitting over my shoulders and tucked my arms and hands into it. "Thank you."

She nodded as if to acknowledge my response. "Name's Friday. Answer my question." There was no glance to see that no one wandered near enough to hear, but there wasn't anyone around. "I know every witch in the city, and most of their relatives. What are you doing here? Mardi Gras? I don't think so. You've got a haunted feel."

"You're a witch?" I leaned in and whispered as I asked the question.

"Are you damaged in some way or just trying to avoid . . ." Friday stopped, and her eyes widened. "This is new. What?"

Entrenched in her shawl, I pulled back when she reached toward my shoulder.

"Stop it," she hissed. Warm fingers touched my neck and she pressed as if probing. "Not a symbiont, that's for sure. But some entity. Not of Earth, or not of our time."

I jerked away and pulled my hands free of the warm shawl. "Don't." *Did you sense anything?*

Nothing, Mistress.

She sensed you.

Yes, Mistress, it seems so.

"What's your name?" Friday asked. Her eyes had grown sharper and more piercing.

"Ahnjii."

"Just Ahnjii?"

"Ahnjii Fate."

Friday pursed her lips and swore. "Just Ahnjii then." She glanced down the street.

She was a witch if she'd sensed that my last name wasn't my true name. Oddly, I didn't feel upset that she knew about Khimmer. Something in Friday's demeanor made me trust her, and I'd been wanting to talk with a witch other than Darren.

"C'mon. I got keys to the art shop, and they won't be here for a couple hours, even on Mardi Gras." She jutted her chin down the street and waited until I started walking to keep pace with me. "I smelled something strange when you started down my street. You've got some trouble on you as well."

"Smelled?" I asked.

Friday studied me. "You're not dim, but how have you managed to stay out of the hands of the Knights or the high Fae? I knew something was in the wind; maybe it's you." She spoke as if to herself. Without warning she turned to a door with a ready key in hand. "I open the door for deliveries sometimes."

Punching numbers into the alarm with one hand, she motioned toward two oval chairs with the other. The room was sparse with a few pictures and a pungent scent that reminded me of Laura's paints.

"Where are you from?" Friday asked before she took the chair beside me.

In the back of my mind, I'd been considering whether I could trust her, and I did. She didn't trust the high Council or Knights, so I doubted it would get back to them. What if she knew about the gate and I could get back home? With Tyler abducted, I felt alone and wanted someone to trust.

"Between us?"

She motioned into the air, exposing some of her tattooed arm as the sleeve dropped. "Unless I think you're a risk to my people."

I wasn't sure who she considered her people, but I meant no one harm, except for Gregor. "I'm from Duruce. A different planet."

"The entity with you is from there as well?"

"Yes." A pair of younger women in hooded coats walked past, peering in. It felt almost warm away from the breeze.

"How'd you get here?" Friday asked.

"A gate. I fell through it and haven't been able to find it again. I've tried."

"Is it closed? Have others come through?"

Could someone have followed me? "I doubt it."

"Which? Answer clearly. Is it closed?"

"I don't see how, but I don't understand how it works."

"Others?" Friday's tone held impatience, but her expression remained impassive.

"I doubt it. They'd have to climb down into a hole and find it."

"Climbing into holes is not that difficult." Her fingers slid up her sleeve on her left arm. "Describe it."

"Five or six spans deep. It was dark. I didn't see much. I'd been poisoned."

She waited, glaring until she spoke. "The gate?"

"Metal and stone. I don't remember much. I was poisoned." I'd said that. She made me a bit nervous with her rapid fire questions. It reminded me of Turben. "I tried to go back, but there were six gates and I ended up here."

"Six?" Friday's lips tightened. "One to Earth, one to your Duruce, and we don't know where the others lead." She blinked, and I realized she hadn't all this time. "Where's this gate?"

"Slovenia."

Friday swore.

I had some sense that she judged me, and found me

lacking, but it did feel good to speak with someone about my situation. Tyler tended to be uncomfortable when we discussed it. From her swearing, I assumed Friday was as well, but in a different, less emotional way. From her comments, I'd been right not to let the Knights or the high Fae know I wasn't from Earth. Tyler had been right. I touched my phone in my pocket but didn't pull it out. I would know when Darren called or Gregor texted.

"Would you teach me about being a witch?" I asked.

Friday rolled her eyes. "Do I look like a schoolmarm?"

Schoolmarm?

Unknown, Mistress. Perhaps a teacher from context, and if I assume, marm is a derivative of ma'am.

Friday's abrasive nature had a certain comfort to it. She had the same no-nonsense behavior as Shailagh, without the sexuality. I didn't want to believe Shailagh had betrayed me, but she might not have had a choice. Part of my positive response to Friday might have been the warmth on my shoulders and some of the chill relieved from being out of the wind.

Guilt flushed my cheeks as I thought about Tyler. I imagined them tied up and stuck in a cold basement like in some detective novel.

Friday sniffed. "Why are you in New Orleans?"

What I had just told her I had only ever told Tyler. There seemed no point in not discussing Gregor. Tired, I would have loved a cup of hot tea. "It started a couple days ago, with an Upre named Gregor Gehrke. Do you know him?"

"Of him. Nasty piece. They all are, but he's about to need a new host." Friday tilted her head and came closest to a smile that I'd seen on her face. "He senses your gifts. Wants a strong witch for his next host."

"Why does he need a new host?"

"A blood cancer the symbiont can't heal, from what I've heard. Ironic." Friday stood. "Coffee?"

I grinned. "Tea?"

"Probably, but I can't say how it's going to taste. It's a pod thingy. Keep going, I can hear you." She headed toward a partition on the other side of her chair.

I told her of the exchange in Railroad Square while a machine chugged. When she brought hot tea, a rich black from the taste, I explained what I could of the arrest and the lawyers. She didn't interrupt until I mentioned Darren.

"What were you thinking? Half-brained," she mumbled into her cup. "No, you don't know the Knights. They're fanatics. If they catch wind about who you really are and your little friend inside . . ." She frowned and shook her head. "The Knights serve a purpose, but they tend to use a hammer when a broom would suffice. They were known as the Bronze Warriors."

"Darren brought me here. He's investigating Gregor right now. I think he's only involved because the high Fae Council told me Gregor was in New Orleans and he thought I'd come out here alone."

I paused as some of Friday's coffee dripped out of her cup. She swore and rubbed it into the wood with her sneaker. "The high Fae? You are daft. They obviously don't know about where you're from, or about your little friend."

I winced. "They don't know about the gate or Duruce, no one does except Tyler. Well, Deanna and John, but they don't really believe me."

Friday wiped her free hand down her face hard enough to stretch out some of the wrinkles. "How have you survived this? I don't mean that as a compliment."

"I made a deal with the high Fae. They let me go and gave me New Orleans, but I owe them a debt."

She did something I hadn't believed possible; Friday laughed. Everything she'd said had been true and her admonishments were warranted, at least with the high Fae. Darren and the other Knight, Flemming, were trying to help me, though.

"I don't care," I said. "Tyler is my closest friend, and it's my fault they're in trouble. Darren is the second Knight to go investigate."

A man walked past the window wearing white robes, a copper cloak, and a crown. I blinked and Friday followed my glance before swearing. "Mardi Gras." She rubbed absently up her sleeve. "This Tyler, a witch?"

I shook my head. "No. Well maybe a little, but they doesn't know it."

She frowned. "What do they know, about you?"

"Pretty much everything. Tyler was with me when I saved John from the wight."

"Tyler kept it quiet?"

"Yes."

She wiped her face "The Knights lost an investigator? There will be a half-dozen in the city by nightfall."

"Two more today. I'm supposed to stay out of the way until they get here." I touched my phone through my shorts. "Darren is going to call me."

"When?"

"I thought by now." The sun had risen higher, lighting the tops of buildings in the street. Some of the people walking by wore bright colors; others carried masks on sticks or cameras.

"Check in with him. Text him. He'll have his phone on vibrate. The Knights are extremists, not idiots. They rarely lose one of their own, which means Gregor has hired serious security. Your friend might be a lost cause. I can't let you sign that contract." Her face remained expressionless. "Your knowledge about a gate to another world melded into an Upre would constitute a risk to my people."

I chilled at the implied threat and finished my tea. Friday appeared too old to be any danger, but I didn't really know what witches could do besides sense things. After all the mistakes I'd been making, I didn't want to take another risk. "Help me then. Give me Gregor's address."

"The family owns at least a dozen properties in New Orleans proper, more outside of it. The Knights obviously have his present whereabouts. Check in with Darren."

I pulled out my phone and texted, "ANY SIGN OF TYLER?" Likely I'd get no response or a harsh reminder to be patient.

The response came quickly, and it could only have been Gregor. "HOW DELIGHTFUL! DARREN DID NOT TELL ME YOU WERE IN NEW ORLEANS. FRENCH QUARTER. SHOOT ME YOUR EXACT LOCATION AND I'LL HAVE MY PEOPLE PICK YOU UP."

CHAPTER 29

I SWALLOWED and showed Friday the message.

She swore while grabbing my phone, yanked the back off it, and pulled free a black and silver square. "I take it that you won't stop." She handed me a blank phone and slid the square into a pocket at the waist of her brown dress. "Until you're dead, or an Upre. I can't let the latter happen."

Her half full cup sat on the small table in front of her, and the aroma of coffee dominated the room. I felt warm. She tugged her pale green shawl around the snake tattooed on her neck and studied me as if she didn't need an answer.

My pulse quickened. What would Friday do to stop me? I had so little knowledge of witches. "There is another option," I said. "I could rescue Tyler, maybe even kill Gregor."

Friday peered at me. "You're a little spit of a thing. Do you have any idea how strong Upre are? Don't even have to attack you, just compel you."

"I'm not defenseless."

"You're telling me the truth, so you believe it. Now, convince me."

She was giving me a chance. Would she help? "I killed a wight. I can't be compelled." I assumed Upre and high Fae used the same magic. She already knew about Khimmer, so showing her Nightarmor wouldn't be much more information.

She interrupted me. "Wights don't compel. They haven't for a very long time."

What did Shailagh call the wight? I thought to Khimmer.

A dominar, Mistress.

"This one had become a dominar. She'd enthralled John and Tyler."

"Verity protected you?"

"That's what Shailagh calls it. My people call it truthsense."

Her eyes darkened. "Do your people have strong abilities?"

"Truthsense is very rare, but not unheard of."

Friday started to say something, then paused before continuing. "Gregor will have armed men in an entrenched position. They took out two Knights."

"I took out a wight in her own cavern, with her thralls."

Friday did not seem impressed. "Alone?"

"With Shailagh."

She stood with her coffee and stared out the window at the crowding street as she drank. "It's too risky."

If she could help, I'd rather have someone who knew the city. The Knights were either arrogant and overconfident, or Gregor did have good defenses. Any help would be useful. Otherwise, I'd be calling Gregor for a ride once I got the phone working again.

I coughed and waited till she glanced back at me.

Left gauntlet, vambrace, and blade.

Yes, Mistress.

Nightarmor poured across my arm to form intricate black armor with gold and silver filigree. The sheath rose up and an engraved hilt grew from it.

Friday snorted. "Pretty. Does it stop bullets?"

"Yes," I said.

Eldritch weapons will pierce Nightarmor, Mistress. Some are stronger than others.

"Mostly. Wildlings shot me twice just last night."

She opened her mouth, in what I assumed was surprise. "How have you survived here? Wildlings don't shoot witches; they tear them in half. Who else have you pissed off?" Friday waved off any response. "What's your plan, barge in, take some shots, and kill his guards, then Gregor?"

I'd probably try and be a bit stealthier than that, but I'd need an address. "I'd scout it out first like Darren was supposed to do." Had Gregor killed the Knight?

"You've killed people before?"

"Previous occupational hazard." I smiled. Tyler had come up with the term, and I liked it.

"You're going to explain that, afterward." She pointed at my arm. "Get rid of that."

Remove.

Nightarmor flowed back into bangles. "You'll help?" I stood and smiled hopefully.

"There's conditions."

"Agreed."

"Are you always this much of an idiot?"

I liked Friday. "When it comes to my friends, yes."

"Lovely. Condition one, I kill you if you become an Upre host."

I couldn't be confident she could succeed, but if it ever

happened, I'd probably agree. "Can you do it before the thing crawls inside me?" I chuckled at my own morbid joke.

"Nope. If you're stupid enough to let it happen when you can stop it, you deserve that pleasure. Give me your arm."

I held out my hand and she pulled up her left sleeve. There seemed to be no skin without ink. I'd seen similar before on Duruce as well as Earth. She flipped my hand over and cupped my knuckles with hers.

Threads of light sparkled in my vision. They lasted less than a second before others replaced them, but they led from midway up her forearm out into the room around us. Some appeared to touch me for a second.

One of her tattoos raised off her arm. A fat-bodied black spider wiggled itself free of creased skin, leaving a pale empty spot. It skittered toward my hand, and I flinched. Friday held me tight.

Mistress?

Shh.

I felt the little legs on my flesh. Light threads traced off it and went nowhere I could see before they were replaced. Shivers crawled up my back, and goosebumps formed on my arm. The tattoo spider appeared as real and full as any I'd ever seen. It spun in a circle on my wrist and squirmed. Legs sank into my skin, and before I could take a breath, it flattened into a tattoo. The white strings disappeared.

This is not wise, Mistress. I can't protect you from that.

Friday released my hand. "You become an Upre, you die. Our little friend will make sure it's quick. I won't say it'll be painless."

With cautious fingers, I rubbed the edges of the spider's legs, but it was just skin and ink. The shivers didn't stop. "How did you do that?"

"It's not a magic used by many in this era. Most witches don't have the strength." She dropped her left sleeve and began rolling her right sleeve up to her bicep.

"What were the threads of light?" I scowled at the spider. Friday could kill me anytime she wanted.

Friday froze. "What did you see?"

I waved in the air from the spider into the room. "Little threads of light that flickered on and off."

She finished rolling her sleeve up. "Hmm." The same lights appeared, focused on a golden shape on the inside her arm. Her eyes focused on mine. "This little friend is in case you get in trouble. He'll listen to you somewhat. Gets a bit frisky under pressure."

The creature that climbed out of her skin was a fist-sized lion with a beak and wings. Fluffy golden feathers covered all but the piercing eyes, yellow beak, and a short-haired section of its rump. Jumping off her arm, it flew straight for my neck with threads of light streaming from it. I would have found it cute and kitten-like if it didn't have such a fierce expression and birdlike talons for front paws.

I flinched when it landed and squirmed when it tickled as it crawled under the shawl. The urge to scratch it off forced me to grab the tails of the borrowed shawl with my hands. A random line of light passed my vision before the winged creature finally settled into place at the back of my neck. "How do I get it to do something?" As small as it was, I didn't expect to need it.

"It'll know when it's time to help." Friday rolled down her sleeve and loosened the collar of her brown dress. Three yellow butterflies fluttered out, streaming with nearly invisible threads. They fluttered about her head before she straightened her clothes. "Now, in your story you said you blocked Gregor when he attacked. Show me how."

I pictured the struggle, brought my fist to my chest, then struck down sharply.

"Hold your arm up." She grabbed it and positioned my hand sideways in front of her face. The butterflies moved to my wrist and settled on the outer edge. I expected them to blend into a tattoo like the spider, but they just sat there, slowly moving their wings. I could feel little feet on my skin. Darker veins of brown threaded into their bright yellow. The strings of light barely showed, but I could see them attach and disappear quickly. Some lines surely went to Friday.

When they fluttered off of my hand, she nodded with satisfaction. "They've got his scent."

"Scent?"

Friday moved toward the door. "Sense of him. Like when you smell another witch. Not really a smell, but that's the best way to describe it." She let the butterflies out into the street.

I couldn't do that. I hadn't been able to make the magic compass work either. There were a lot of things I couldn't do with my abilities. "Shouldn't we follow them?"

"I've got them. I'd rather they get a little ahead of us with the parades. I'll need to reroute us depending on where Gregor is. They're heading west, and that means closed roads today." She turned and inspected my clothes. "There will be people looking for you on the street. We'll need a disguise, and today is a good day for that."

A woman passed on the street holding a masquerade stick mask with a long pointy beak. Off her shoulders she had a red and green cape, but otherwise she wore only a red bathing suit and boots.

Khimmer, can you do the mask?

Yes, Mistress.

Nightarmor formed across my left arm into a black stick ending in a silver replica of the mask. I pulled it off and held it over my face. "How about this?" The beak protruded, reflecting the colors of the room in a distracting manner.

Friday grunted and tightened her lips. I took it as disapproval.

Cape?

Nightarmor flowed down my back in thin flexible metal with oxidized copper green on one shoulder and burnished copper on the other.

Friday nodded. "Tuck the braid in. Match the boots and jewelry. Choker to beads."

I slipped my hair under the cloak and didn't need to prompt Khimmer as bangles and armbands changed to green and brownish orange.

"Good job. I'm betting your little friend is smarter than you."

Probably.

Yes, Mistress.

I scowled. "Can we go?"

Friday sighed. "Yes, against my best judgment. Your little friend might be smarter than me." She opened the door and motioned me out. "When we get close we'll slow down and circle about, take pictures like good tourists, and let my butterflies gather as much information as they can. Gregor will have people watching the perimeter."

I'd taken many days preparing for an assassination, but I didn't think Tyler had that kind of time. "We're going in today, right?"

"We?" Friday closed the door behind us and locked it. "I'm finding a nice bistro and having brunch while you sort out this mess."

CHAPTER 30

I HAD LESS visibility than I would have liked and kept peeking around the edges of the mask as we walked on the sidewalk. Music played in some areas, either from apartment windows or musicians along the street. Incense, cigarettes, sea salt, and sharper aromas mixed with exhaust to create a unique city odor. What Friday called the French Quarter had the unique architecture I'd noticed earlier. The density of people grew with each block, and the costumes became more garish.

The sun had risen, and with Friday's shawl under my cloak, I was warm. The people appeared in a celebratory mood, even intoxicated. My chest was tight, though I kept a pleasant smile for the world.

Louder music echoed ahead of us and to our right. "That's the parade on Saint Charles." Where we walked, most of the pedestrians crossed in front of us toward the direction she pointed.

A crowd formed at the end of a cross street two blocks from us. Cars still drove past, but the foot traffic died off between intersections. Friday studied everyone as intently as I did. Most appeared to have some business there even if they were just sweeping up dead leaves. Down one of the side streets, someone lit a firework that shrieked and ended in a bang.

"He's set up people around his building on two sides."

I assumed Friday referred to Gregor. "How approachable are the other two directions?"

We crossed the street toward a park. "One is an occupied residence, the other a fenced-in church." Wiping leaves away with her sneaker, she drew a square with her toe and began mapping out Gregor's building. "His people outside the grounds are stationed in a third-floor apartment overlooking the front, an obvious sedan right outside the gate, an RV in the parking lot on the side street, and a spotter in a building across from the church."

It would be hard to get a visual on the building before I approached it. "Have you — they — found Tyler?"

Friday scrubbed her map clear with her toe. "No. Nor Gregor." We walked for nearly the length of the park before she cleared leaves again. "Three-story main house. Two guards on the second floor. Three on the ground floor. Garage is empty except for vehicles." She rubbed down her face which I took as an expression of concern. "Three in the back yard." She tapped three spots. Eight visible hired security. Might be more. They'll be top notch, ex-military."

I stepped behind the map. "Church?"

"Yes." I'd come in from that side, the back of Gregor's house.

She rubbed the markings away, and we continue down the sidewalk. Friday kept a leisurely pace that I fought to maintain. Assuming her drawings were aligned to our position, shadows would be to my advantage behind the garage. My pulse pounded despite our stroll.

In a few blocks, Friday turned us right and then left, finally stopping us as if we were having a conversation. "Next corner on the right."

A two-story white building had columns rising up the front. The architecture of this neighborhood had changed, and Gregor's building stood out. We continued the process three times, giving me some views of the building from different angles. The parade no longer sounded nearby. People had begun to wander back into the neighborhood from the blockaded street. The crowd, despite their laughing and levity, made me more tense.

Friday stopped us, and people wove around us. "Shawl?" She put out her hand. It had grown warm. "I'd hate to see it get ruined."

I slid the cloth out from under my cape. We were on the opposite side of the block from Gregor's house, but his people could be among the crowd. Once I had the element of surprise, I would be more comfortable. "Where will you be?"

"Café a couple blocks down on Jackson, the two lane road." She gestured behind us before she turned to leave me. "I'll catch up with you, if you make it."

I strode a little quicker than Friday had been. We would make it, Tyler and me.

The street on the backside of Gregor's block was still cordoned off for cars, but brightly dressed pedestrians crossed through barricades, and the police let them. Others waited on the sidewalks and drank. Friday had mentioned a second parade, but I had no sense of time except we were past morning bells. A heavy stench of exhaust hung at the crowded main street with added notes of cigarettes and alcohol.

My mask still held in place, I scanned the faces I could. Surveillance had to be tightest close to Gregor's house, but there were a lot of women my age. I slowed my pace to tag behind a loose group of three women dressed in little more than fur boots and short bright skirts. All the buildings on Gregor's block seemed large, and one had been turned into a motel with a long canopy out to the street. The last on the corner had an awning for cars that I recognized as a bank.

I turned into the driveway and passed under the empty arches. No people stood at the large windows of the bank.

Anyone following?

I don't believe so, Mistress. There are a lot of people.

The church stood behind the parking lot of the bank, and beyond that the house with Gregor and Tyler.

A large dumpster blocked me from the noisy side street, so I drew close to it. The church rose from trees ahead. The fence between the bank parking lot and the back of the church was old, stained wood a head taller than myself. Once I reached the back of the church, I'd have to react and respond to whatever lay between me and Gregor's house. The best Friday had been able to give me was a low brick wall and a high hedge.

I turned to the main street, where people were still thick, and crouched at the dumpster. Horns played from somewhere, echoing down the streets. No one purposefully looked in my direction; there was too much to see. *Replace all, full climbing gear.*

Yes, Mistress.

Nightarmor enclosed me in a flexible suit of black metal that fit my skin tighter than a hoodie. Presently, I only need to climb a fence or two, but the construction made for excellent mobility. Khimmer's vision replaced mine. Strangely dressed for the celebration, I raced for the church's fence. The voices in the street to my left remained conversational and not alarmed, but I didn't look, hoping they were self-absorbed.

I leaped, grabbed the wobbly top of the fence, and spun, clearing the wood and dropping into an empty parking lot shaded by trees. I could see one window of Gregor's house over the dark untrimmed hedge. His spotter across the street likely had a good view down the drive, but not the back parking lot. The windows of the church were dark.

No orange shape waited at Gregor's upstairs window, so I raced to the back of the church, reached the corner, and took a careful look across the street. Unkempt brush blocked much of my view until I stepped closer to the drive and a mere two steps from Gregor's wall.

The small garden waited on the other side. Through the brick and hedge, I could make out the three orange shapes of the guards, exactly where Friday had detailed them.

Across the street, an orange haze showed a woman in an upper window. She focused on the revelers milling down the street.

I took two steps, leaped sideways to the wall, and landed on the top hidden under the sprawling hedge. The branches rustled, and I watched the closest man turn to peer directly at me.

My pulse pounded with exertion and excitement. I stared back, knowing I was dull black and under the shade of branches. Higher pitched horns joined the music and breathed as the guard returned to his stance. He wore a pad of body armor, dulling some of his orange shape. His hands crossed at his groin where he held a weapon.

Under the hedge was mulch, and the man stood on

quiet grass. The man on the far corner of the lawn faced the front of the house, and a woman stood guard on the side. Inside, a vague form milled near the back door. Along with the aroma of soil and mulch, I smelled a dead body and hoped it was not Darren. I didn't wish him harm.

My left hand already rested on my hip. *Left plumbata.*

Yes, Mistress. There was no mistaking Khimmer's reluctance in their tone. They hated when I risked their metal to throwing weapons. The small heavy dart formed at the edge of my fingers.

Dory.

The shaft rose over my shoulder into the dry branches of the hedge. Right hand and right toe stiff on the wall, I lifted my left leg and dropped it silently to the mulch before letting it take my weight. Facing the back of the closest guard, I had the garage to my back, and the man I assumed had been Flemming lay in the gardens to my left.

I focused on the woman watching the far side and the guard inside by the back door. When they both appeared to be looking away, I threw the dart past the man closest to me.

The plumbata sank into the neck of the man who stood at the corner of the garden.

Tracing the trajectory, the guard in front of me turned as I expected. His gun rose as he moved, but his surprise gave me a moment's edge. With a mid-shaft grip, I swung the sharp tip of the spear from my back and through his throat in a single one-handed swipe.

Neither body had settled to the grass as I sprinted for the back corner of the house where the woman guarded the side. Visible to all windows on the top floor, I could only hope they focused on the crowds of noisy parade watchers that filled the streets around us.

The playing horns let out a long mournful note as I

jabbed the spear forward. I had a grip a hands-width from the end of the shaft as I stopped three steps away from the dying woman. The tip caught her under the ear behind the jaw. She hadn't even spotted me yet. In three breaths, I'd cleared the back garden without raising an alarm.

Remove spear. Full armor. Sword.

As it reformed, Nightarmor poured out of the dying woman, letting blood flow freely.

I wouldn't have long before someone from inside spotted the bodies in the yard. Trampling low brush, I pressed face first against the side of the house beside the window. The orange shape closest to me was another woman; she would be the first to see the bodies through the glass doors in the back.

Another guard waited at the front door, and a third dimmer shape stood at the back near the garage. Five shapes waited above on the second floor. Three were prone and two paced. One would be Tyler.

Scaling spikes.

Yes, Mistress.

Nightarmor formed barbs out my thumbs, forefingers, and heels. Grabbing the corner of the building, I dug into the light stucco that covered it. A decorative lip formed above, dividing the two stories. It appeared wide enough to stand on. If I could get Tyler out without a battle, then I'd deal with Gregor another day. The horn playing ended, leaving only the discordant buzz of the crowds in the street.

This high up, the hedges wouldn't hide me. If someone on the street or the neighbors called the police, it might be either a helpful distraction or more guns.

The closest prone shape lay just inside the back window. I sidled along the decorative edge and glimpsed inside through a flimsy curtain.

Darren lay on the floor beside a door open to a walkway and staircase. His hat was gone, and zip ties clamped around his ankles and wrists. I could see little else through the fabric, but his eyes weren't open.

The doorbell rang from downstairs, and Gregor swore from another room.

CHAPTER 31

I SHIFTED out of sight from the window, focusing on the now quickly moving shapes. One of the prone figures had risen and moved for the stairs; Gregor, I assumed.

One tall figure, the shape and gait indicating a woman, moved into the room with Darren, then left and closed the door. She moved toward the center of the building. A short breeze brought salt air to dominate the other city scents. My pulse pounded in my ears with anticipation.

The last unidentified prone figure near the front of the building shifted erratically. That would be Tyler. Conscious and alive. I eased a light breath out and returned to the window. The doorbell rang a second time. Gregor's voice echoed inside.

Short blade.

Holding onto the shutter for leverage, I splintered through wood as I slid the lock open with the blade's tip. This construction didn't vary between Earth and Duruce. I kept the knife in hand while I pushed up the window with a too-thick gauntleted finger. It slid easily, and Darren didn't shift or open his eyes. With Khimmer's vision, I knew the Knight remained alive.

Gregor barked commands while he walked down the stairs, and I slid into Darren's richly decorated prison. The room smelled falsely of flowers. Darren didn't stir when I touched his shoulder. The blood on his sleeve came from a wound on his left shoulder. They'd taken his leather jacket and hat. I cut the zip ties. His arms dropped to his side, and the toes of his boots swayed apart. Unless I had time while rescuing Tyler, that was the most I would do to help. If he'd been conscious, it would have been another matter. I sheathed the short knife on my left vambrace.

Gregor had reached the bottom floor. The tall guard stood halfway down the stairs. A second waited in the room with Tyler. Those on the bottom floor clustered near the front. The distraction, whether police or some passerby who'd seen me scaling the walls, was perfectly timed.

Through Khimmer's vision I focused on the house's construction that lay between the door to Darren's room and the guards. It had a disorienting affect when I used their sight this way, but I believed I could open the door without being seen. If I could get to the one guard near Tyler, I might be out of the house before they realized what I'd done. I still hadn't drawn my sword. Stealth and surprise were my ally.

Glove, right palm.

Nightarmor shifted to soft flexible metal in the palm of my right gauntlet up to the fingertips, making for a quieter grip on the doorknob. I could hear better after I opened the door the slightest crack.

A second voice greeted Gregor, familial and friendly. Not the police. If it were a neighbor, they did not sound excited or scream, "There's someone breaking into the second floor." Luck remained on my side. I couldn't gauge whether the top of the door was in sight of the guard on the stairs, but she seemed focused on the commotion at the front door.

I pulled the door slowly open, though it hadn't creaked earlier when the guard closed it. With my right foot and hip sliding through the opening, the tall woman on the stairs yelled out an alarm.

Hades. I dashed through the door and yanked it closed.

She stepped backward up the steps, weapon raised. The stairwell started just to my left and swept down to the corner landing behind her. The balcony still kept me from her line of sight, but I would be visible to her in moments. Three doors waited to my right, one with a prone figure and a second form just on the other side of the door.

I crouched as I ran. My boots clattered on polished wood and echoed in the stairwell. The conversation below had stopped.

Pulling my sword, I raced for the door where they held Tyler. A muted gunshot fired, and a small blister formed on the back of my left arm as Nightarmor absorbed the impact. A second seared my hip. The third splintered wood behind me, possibly a balustrade. As the door opened a hands-width, I thrust my blade through the wooden door into the face of the guard. Blade, body, and door shoved into the room and wedged for a second before Khimmer melted the tip free.

A fourth bullet burned the small of my back, and I barely heard the gunshot.

Mistress!

I jumped over the body through the doorway, taking one of the next two shots with a blister to the back of my thigh. Inside the helmet, I imagined the smell of burning flesh.

My heart raced, anticipation and concern battling for dominance.

Their weapons are suppressed, but still too powerful for sustained protection, Mistress.

Burns dotted the lower half of my body. Gagged, Tyler wriggled on an ornate bed. There were zip ties around their wrists, and their ankles were bound to a chain of zip ties anchored to the carved wooden posts. Tyler's eyes were wide, and their expression flickered between anger and panic. Muffled, Tyler yelled.

I slammed the door shut and punched the handle askew with my fist. There were no bolts or locks. Two bullets punched through the bottom panel of the door, one blistering my right shin. Voices were yelling in the stairwell below. Tyler screamed through the gag.

Dancing back to Tyler, I slashed twice to cut through the zip ties linking their hands to the posts, then tossed the short blade onto the bed.

I turned to face the door, sword ready while Tyler freed themself. The commotion downstairs continued. The room had a window on the front of the house, so I might be able to lower Tyler to the ground.

"Ahnjii, stop." Tyler's voice was ragged, deep, and dry with a tone of desperation. "I'm wired to explode. This is a trap."

The bullets had ceased. Two voices argued downstairs, and the louder haughty tone was surely Gregor's. Every blister throbbed. I hadn't slept in a day, and I felt it crashing down on me as I turned.

The blade remained on the beige comforter where I'd tossed it. Tyler had not moved, except to bring a hand up to slide down the gag. With a finger, Tyler pointed toward a thin metal choker that I'd missed. Outside the window in the street, people were laughing and continuing their holiday revelry. The crowds were oblivious to what was happening inside Gregor's house.

Khimmer, can we cut it?

I doubt it, Mistress. I do not understand the technology. I am untrained in these matters. I do not suggest taking the risk.

My mouth felt gummy, and my heart beat in my throat. *That's it, Gregor wins.* I wouldn't let Tyler explode. I imagined the strange symbiont crawling inside me and didn't shiver.

Try to think of way to get it off Tyler, or make it not work.

Yes, Mistress.

I had one consolation, I'd die the moment afterward. As if in a dream, I turned my arm, looking at the armor and the spider tattoo that hid under it. If it saved Tyler, then I could accept this.

Khimmer, if I die, what will you do?

Unknown, Mistress. Protocols do not exist for outside of Duruce.

"I'm sorry," I said to Tyler.

"We're both going to die," Tyler said. "I've been lying here waiting and trying to think a way out of this."

Tyler knew nothing of Friday, and I would have loved to explain if the situation were different. I turned back to the door. Blood stained the hole my sword had left; dark rivulets ran down the polished wood. Drops pooled on the floor.

I closed my eyes and rested my blade on my shoulder. "I've got to go now." I'd get Gregor's promise that Tyler would survive.

The door handle fell off in my hand, and I couldn't help

but laugh. I took a step back and kicked the door open. Every blister complained.

The tall woman had a new friend, a glowering man with a shaved head. They aimed their overly long weapons at me. I strolled out with a bitter smile hidden inside my helmet. I could see the others clustered as orange shapes underneath me. Darren hadn't moved. I'd try and negotiate his life as well.

I took the first step, and the two guards pressed against the wall at the landing.

Gregor stood behind a squat man who had two weapons, one with a long barrel like the others, and a second shorter gun with a muzzle I could have put my finger inside. Behind Gregor was a solid man who could have been a cowboy. He was likely the unwelcome guest. A lanky guard with the telltale bulky vest held the cowboy's bicep firmly.

I paused, almost missing the redder shape at the cowboy's chest. Another Upre, but restrained by a guard. I studied Gregor who had a smug smile; it seemed he'd won that argument as well.

My boot heel clacked as I continued down to the next step. The noise outside had lessened, the crowd thinning. My sword remained on my shoulder as I passed the two guards. Gregor waited.

The cowboy indeed had a slight drawl. "This ain't going to go over well, Gregor. Lot of families are going to be in an uproar, yours included." His brown hair poked from under a tan western hat that sat slightly askew, as if from a struggle.

Gregor didn't take his eyes off me. "I'll ask forgiveness, once it's done."

"Because you would never get permission."

"Shut up, Benjamin."

Benjamin's guard poked the muzzle of his weapon against the cowboy's ribs, aimed directly at the symbiont inside. I hadn't expected these guards to know what kind of creatures they worked for. I was surprised that one of the Upre stood up for me, but the high Fae had seemed to have difficulty believing Gregor's behavior as well.

I watched the Upre guest as I took the next step. Could he convince Gregor to end this? I doubted it, but any hope was better than none.

Khimmer interrupted my thoughts. *There is electrical storage inside the device, Mistress. I can drain it if I slightly alter the structure of the knife you left.*

Will that stop the bomb from exploding? New hope lightened my chest.

I believe so, Mistress. I must warn you that without knowledge of the construction, it could also detonate it.

Stumbling, I nearly tripped on a step. I'd rather negotiate with my life. Gregor's eyes were cold and still managed to gleam with the excitement of his win. In his right hand he held a pile of papers, the contract I assumed. The left hand hid behind the guard.

Don't.

Yes, Mistress.

Gregor had bested me with an Earth technology that I didn't understand. We didn't have bombs or guns on Duruce. The concept had been explained by Tyler themself when I'd read about it in one of their books. It all tied into cars, bullets, and war in a confusing way. We'd bought fireworks. My bitter smile returned.

The foyer spread out behind jubilant Gregor, the sun shining in the front door and windows. The guard remained between us, just to the side, weapons pointed down. My sword remained on my shoulder.

I'd start with Tyler, then work down to Darren. "Tyler gets to leave here, no more harmed than they are now."

"Of course," Gregor lied.

CHAPTER 32

I staggered at his lie.

Gregor swore. His self-satisfied look died with his words. The guard in front of him barely moved, but both of his weapon barrels raised to point at my knees.

My pulse raced, and my fist tightened on my sword. Gregor planned to kill Tyler. "You've got to let him go."

Benjamin spoke calmly as if were selecting ingredients for a bowl of Pho. "Need to add it to the contract. A guarantee of your friend's life."

"Shut up, Benjamin." With a grimace, Gregor snarled at the other Upre.

"I didn't come here without others knowing. This ain't all wrapped up neat and nice like you're thinking."

Gregor waved his contract at Benjamin as if to sweep the words away, then yelled at the guard while pointing the papers toward a door. "Get him out of here. The garage." His other hand held a small device wrapped in a white-knuckled fist.

Benjamin let himself be pushed out, though he kept his eyes on me.

Gregor shook himself as the door closed. "Take off that helmet so I can see your eyes."

"Tyler goes free."

"I can't take that risk." His face tightened, then looked hopeful. "You can decide after we're integrated. That, I'll agree to. You might not care, but you'll be in charge after the symbiont changes hosts. This afternoon."

What would I be when I was a host to a symbiont? A puppet? It didn't matter. Friday's tattoo mandated that I make this deal beforehand. I would have to wait until Tyler was out the door before agreeing. That would be difficult. Gregor couldn't be sure that I wouldn't slice my way out of the situation. Did Gregor know about Nightarmor? I could give him the sword to show my compliance. Why did the symbiont invasion have to happen this afternoon?

"In the contract." I couldn't be sure why I trusted Benjamin.

Gregor trembled with rage and threw the contract across the polished wood floor. "I don't need a contract."

I sensed him.

Like a burning on my soul, he exposed my emotions with white hot light. Then it twisted, even though I knew it for a lie. Like a beating sun on a Tallahassee afternoon, his magic burned ever brighter. I knew that he manipulated something, but a part of me wanted to accept a warped promise of comfort and power.

I shuffled on the steps. Turben would never beat me in sparring again. ¶The Aegis monks were a distant memory. I was free to choose sex and friends at will. Shailagh, Laura, and Vivianne. Friendships would have no hold on me; I would outlive them all. Perhaps even Woo.

I had a duty to Nyx and Queen that would never end. They trapped me as surely as anyone.

King Dior lived happily never knowing judgment. I'd failed.

Joined, I would have no need to worry about any of it. I just had to accept my new life. This was not peace, but power. Combined, we would be unstoppable. Darren would be the next of many Knights to die. Nightarmor would protect us.

Mistress! Khimmer pushed through, and I knew that they'd been trying. I hadn't been able to fully hear them.

I knew Gregor's lies. It wouldn't have mattered; Friday's plans would have stopped it all. If I had more time, I would have liked to make friends with her.

Gregor would kill Tyler, or his people would if I trapped him in a dead host.

He raised his clenched fist. "I did not understand this armor fully, until now. I may have miscalculated." Gregor frowned, but his eyes shone with greed. "I can agree to keep Tyler alive."

Truth.

Gregor wanted Nightarmor.

Will you remain with my body?

I believe so, Mistress. It betrayed everything the Aegis monks stood for. "Tyler will go free?"

Gregor's lips tightened.

Would he just hold Tyler hostage? He'd tried to trick me. Tyler had one chance to survive. *Do it. Drain the device.*

I waved my left hand out, partially to distract the three guards surrounding me. "If Tyler's alive, we could continue the discussion, afterward."

Hope lit Gregor's face. "Yes, exactly."

Done, Mistress.

I sliced the guard in front of me from chin to groin. "Run, Tyler! It's disabled!"

The squat guard managed his shots even as he realized his death. His larger gun flashed white and deafened me in my helmet.

Mistress!

My left knee blistered, but my right leg spun outward with the impact. Pain seared my mind, and I couldn't hold my weight. The leg buckled, and I clattered to the stairs, sliding a step. My ears rang in my helmet, barely registering as it smacked against wood behind me.

I never let go of my sword. The guard slid toward the floor, legs buckling and insides loosening. His two guns had dropped and spun slowly.

Gregor's face showed his surprise. As he took a step back, a black and red tube that looked like a cigarette lighter dropped from his hand.

A step pressed my head forward, and I felt Friday's fluffy friend pushing through Nightarmor's vent at the back. What would the little flying creature do?

I smiled through the pain as Gregor looked from the device rattling on wood to the bedroom on the second floor. I tensed, preparing to rise on my good leg. There was no explosion.

Tyler?

Freeing themself, Mistress.

Thank you, Khimmer.

Bullets rained on the top of my helmet and pauldrons. They kept to a rapid alternating rhythm, and blisters speckled my head and shoulders. I could smell burnt hair. How long could Khimmer hold them off? On one leg, it would be a tough battle up the stairs to the landing.

I had my left elbow positioned on a step as the gunshots

continued, but the bullets didn't reach me. Distant, through the ringing in my ears, I could hear them hit something with wet dull thuds.

A golden hind paw, larger than my head, pressed against my right shoulder and shoved me down the stairs, into the splayed guard. My right boot wedged against the corpse's leg, and pain sparkled Khimmer's vision with white stars.

Feathers drifted past, then vanished.

Gregor backed up with wide eyes. He glanced from me to Friday's creature, then to the wide barreled gun that had broken my knee. Grimacing and determined, he leaped forward and reached for the gun lying in the spreading pool of blood. I might not survive another shot from that weapon.

The woman screamed wetly behind me and then stopped short.

I shoved on a step with my left hand, pushing my torso off the steps and sliding up the railing with my right shoulder. *Tyler?* I shuffled my left boot back, arching my body up while my right leg screamed.

Coming this way, Mistress.

No. I couldn't look. "Run, Tyler!"

Gregor stood in the growing puddle of blood and fumbled with the slick weapon. If he fired before I could stand and swing, then I might never stand again. He gained a grip and raised the muzzle.

I didn't have the reach and wouldn't make it to a stance.

Mistress!

Dory.

Nightarmor's tip elongated, and as it lengthened, I shoved the sharp tip into the muzzle, up to the shaft. Khimmer adjusted to fit. I could only hope that the bullet couldn't come out if I blocked the barrel. I flinched as Gregor's finger pulled the trigger.

The spear shot backward out of my grasp. The vibration of metal on metal tingled on my fingertips. White-hot fire engulfed the gun. Metal clanked against my left shoulder, and I winced. I thought I'd failed, but it didn't blister. Deafened by the explosion, I could only hear echoes of my pulse pounding.

Nightarmor's spear turned into a liquid rivulet of metal. Shining black liquid chased my gauntlet as I fell back to the stairs. Gregor's face bled as he toppled. A cloud of smoke rose from where the gun had been.

Tyler stood at the railing above, two steps back from where Darren paused at the top of the stairs.

Dying or dead, Gregor began to fade in Khimmer's vision. A gruesome hole gaped where his right ear and temple had been. The symbiont glowed brighter than the rest of the host body. The weapon was nowhere to be seen, but one of Gregor's fingers had landed on the step below me.

A flash of relief twitched at my lips. Still, I had to assume the symbiont would live. My chest hurt when I blew out a breath; I needed to finish and get us out of this house. I couldn't relax until Tyler was safe.

Wincing, I tried to twist around, to see where the bald guard was. The roaring in my ears disoriented my senses. The room sounded empty and still, like we were safe. We weren't; Darren and Tyler stood in the open. I hadn't gone through all this to have Tyler shot.

With more effort than expected, I managed an elbow on a step. I flinched when a shaved head bounced past and rolled to rest on Gregor's right arm. The neck of the guard looked pinched and flattened at the edges. The eyes were wide and stared off to the side.

Sagging, I forced myself to roll so my left knee braced on a step. We still had to deal with the other Upre and Gregor's guard inside. There were more of Gregor's people in the street outside; surely they'd heard the commotion.

Friday's little creature had somehow grown to the size of a cow. Most of its wings were gone, as if they been erased. It only had one front claw; the other ended abruptly at a knobby knuckle, and a rear paw had been damaged with missing toes. Sharp black eyes glared up at Darren.

"Whoa there, Fluffy. Friends. Friends." I reached out a hand, as if to reassure Friday's tattoo beast and gestured toward Tyler and Darren.

I twisted with a grimace and turned, my right leg painfully uncooperative. With one hand on a step and the other gripping the railing, I was able to stand on one leg facing up the stairs. "You okay?" I asked Tyler. They held my short blade but still had zip ties on their wrists like cheap bracelets.

Tyler said something, but I couldn't hear well enough to make any sense. Friday's creature stood on the woman's corpse and the headless body of the male guard. Its eyes darted around the room "Fluff." I gestured down the stairs toward Gregor. "Can you make some room for my friends to come down?"

CHAPTER 33

I GLANCED between the unmoving beast and the people I needed to get out of the building. The smell of burnt hair stunk inside my helmet, and I wanted my armor off, but we weren't done.

My pulse rate had slowed, but we wouldn't be safe until we were far from this house. My hearing was beginning to return.

Friday's creature eyed me. It no longer looked cute and fluffy considering its beak, eyes, and pieces torn away by gunfire. I would have to thank the witch for her help.

"Come on. You're done. Take a break." I didn't have time to wait for the rest of Gregor's men to come and find that I'd killed their boss, or the host of their boss. I doubt they'd quibble about the situation before they began shooting.

Launching off one foot, the golden creature leaped toward me.

"Hades." I shifted but was in no position to move out of the way.

Mid-leap it snapped back into a fistful of feathers before

it scrabbled to a landing on my pauldron. I swallowed my heart as it burrowed back through Nightarmor's vent and tickled my neck. I took a breath, turned to Tyler and Darren, and smiled reassuringly under my helmet.

"The guard will be alright." Benjamin walked into the room behind me, and I nearly lost the footing I'd gained. He was looking at Gregor's body. He spoke loud enough that I could hear him over the roaring echo. "Those last couple of shots might bring in some locals. NOLA police don't fancy gunfire, even during Mardi Gras." His accent masked the significance of his words, forcing me to pause.

Darren spoke with a muted, raspy voice from the top of the stairs. "You know what he was trying to do? That he killed a Knight?"

Benjamin grimaced and adjusted his hat. "Didn't know about you losing one of yours. Sorry. Quite a mess." He pulled out his phone and called someone. "All clear?"

If someone replied, I couldn't hear it. I couldn't blindly trust Benjamin, but he wasn't trying to kill me, and that seemed to be a good sign.

"No problems?" He winked and gave me a thumbs up. "All right. Have one of the boys take a walk down the next block and fire off a round. Something loud. A 357 ought to do. Then have them skedaddle. The rest of you stay put 'til I can get this hammered out with family." He hung up and gestured in a circle. "I think we've got all Gregor's people rounded up and tied down." He tilted his hat off his head. "Sorry about all this, Ma'am. Gregor's always been a bad hoss, if you know what I mean."

I didn't understand much of what Benjamin had said, but he seemed to be helping us.

"We're going to demand some oversight on the new

transition," Darren insisted. "I'm assuming the symbiont will survive."

Benjamin glanced at Gregor's body. "Yeah, we're all going to have a bit to say to Gregor's family. I'll add you to the list. I'll be a witness to Gregor's mishaps. I knew something was brewing, just didn't get the gist until the end. You were just defending yourself, that's for sure. It's a bad box all around, but you all don't need to worry." He motioned to my leg. "You look like you'll need to get that looked at."

"We'll keep you as point of contact, then. I don't know who they'll assign." Darren's voice had shifted to behind me, and I turned to find him picking up a gun lying beside the dead woman. Her throat had been collapsed on one side as if pinched by something sharp. I remembered Fluffy's beak and grimaced.

Tyler picked their way down the steps as if unwilling to pass through the trail of bodies. There was no other way out, and I couldn't climb up the blood-slick steps with one leg. We needed to get someplace we felt safe. I could trust Benjamin to a certain degree, from what I understood, but I'd be happier to be home where Laura could heal my knee.

Darren passed me with a quick glance. My eyeless helmet could be intimidating. He held the procured weapon in his right hand, the side of which he held pressed against a wound in his left shoulder. The blood on the shirt looked too wet.

Detach helmet.

Yes, Mistress.

I pulled off the helmet, unsure whether Benjamin had any idea about Nightarmor. Would Gregor's symbiont know or remember? Like the debts I'd piled up, that would have to wait for the future. The air didn't smell any better than my burnt hair. I wasn't going to be able to stand much longer.

"You okay?" I asked Tyler.

My comment seemed to stir Tyler into a determined movement. "No. I'm angry and terrified."

Darren started to speak, and I raised a hand and helmet in his direction. "Tyler's not going to post about this on the internet. They know what you'll do."

Tyler's lip trembled, and I sensed the rage. They wouldn't look at the woman's hand sprawled on the landing, but they stepped over it. When they reached me, Tyler placed their forehead on mine. "Thank you. Are you okay?"

"Nothing that can't be fixed," I hoped.

"Can we leave now?" Tyler whispered. I felt a level of terror resting in them. What had Gregor threatened? The thin black collar still hung around their neck.

How do I get this off? I thought to Khimmer.

There's a slide latch on your left, Mistress.

I let go of the railing and balanced on my good leg, removing the device and tossing it with the bodies on the landing. Tyler shivered. "Now we can go," I said.

Benjamin's eyes followed the device before studying me. I wasn't about to explain.

"Thank you." Tyler looked into my eyes, and their lips moved as if they might say something more. They shook slightly with an odd expression, and I couldn't tell whether they were going to laugh or sob. Tyler studied my eyes, then leaned forward and gave me a gentle but prolonged kiss.

My heart fluttered as I responded, but Tyler ended it too quickly.

We were just friends.

CHAPTER 34

I swayed on the stairs, looking away from Tyler. My cheeks flushed. I focused on Gregor's mangled body.

Do you think you can get us to Friday?

Yes, Mistress. I understood her directions.

My body sagged from exhaustion and the relief of the skirmish at an end. The desire to be somewhere else, preferably home with Tyler, weighed against my injured leg and the uncertainty of what I needed to do next.

The stink of burnt hair mixed with the reek of the blood and death. I still could hear the ringing in my ears from the oversized gun that had killed Gregor's host.

Tyler looked awkward, either from the kiss or the litter of dead bodies.

"Let me cut those off." I motioned toward the zip ties around Tyler's wrist and my blade in their hands.

"Yeah." Tyler pinched my blade high on the hilt and offered it to me.

A blue spark snapped from the knife to my gauntlet when I touched it. Darren and Benjamin turned at the sound, and Tyler nearly dropped the blade before I had the hilt firmly in hand. I assumed it had been part of Khimmer's draining of the device, but I wasn't about to discuss it.

I held the helmet with index finger and thumb while the remaining fingers pressed against the railing for support. Carefully and deftly, I cut the zip ties from Tyler's trembling wrists. "You okay?"

Tyler's glance flicked to the bodies on the landing above us. "No. Not at all. No one should be okay with any of this."

I flushed at their assertion. A part of me always had remorse, but I would not spare one of the dead on the floor if it meant risking Tyler. I sheathed the blade.

Can you make it easier for me to walk? I thought to Khimmer.

Yes, Mistress.

Pain howled in my knee as Nightarmor stiffened, straightening the leg and pinching tight at my hip. I grimaced, but the agony subsided, and when I put weight on it to go down the stairs, I felt no pressure on my knee.

"Y'all need to get some medical care. Hospital for the lady, but . . ." Benjamin tilted his head toward Darren. "You got someone who can care for a gunshot wound? If not, I got people."

Darren looked paler than usual, but his expression had gotten darker and more determined. "Find my phone or Flemming's, and I'll get someone here."

I took a tentative step, holding the rail with my right hand, ready to leave. Benjamin's phone rang; he answered it and swore immediately. "We got company on the doorstep."

Darren stepped over the blood on the floor, heading for the entry.

It would be impossible not to see the man I'd nearly split in half or his blood. Gregor and the snipped free bald head were a pace behind that. Pieces of flesh and gun were splattered all across the floor where blood had sprayed in fine droplets from the exploding weapon. Opening the front door would allow anyone to see the carnage.

The door opened and Friday walked in. She scanned the room and pursed her lips, waving off Darren and his gun. "I'm here to pick up my kid," she said to Benjamin, closing the door quickly behind her.

Benjamin spoke into his phone. "It's okay."

Friday circled around Darren as she inspected the bodies. "Symbiont still alive." She didn't ask a question. Her eyes flicked to me and Tyler, but then she focused on Benjamin. "Your people outside?"

He nodded and peered as intently at her as she did him. "You helping them?" Benjamin asked, poking a thumb toward me.

"Kids are under my care. Yes." She nudged her chin at Gregor. "He's not one of your family. What are you doing here?"

Benjamin almost smiled. "Sticking my nose where it don't belong. I got wind he was dealing some quick and dirty cards. I don't like the attention that could bring."

Friday relaxed and took a longer look at me and Tyler. "You never did fit well with your family, either. Black sheep." I assumed she was still talking about Benjamin.

"Odd stick, they might say."

She spun with a step and faced Darren. "You look to be hurt the worst, of the living." He flinched when she started peeling back his shirt to expose an ugly wound in his armpit. Blood smeared her fingertips. "You okay if I slow this down?"

Darren's face tightened, then he sighed. "There's still a round in there."

Friday swore. "I can see that. It's going to hurt. Want to lie down?"

He shook his head, and immediately I saw the bright fibers string from her hand. At this distance I could see where some attached for a moment to me, Benjamin, and even the dead. Other lines of light shot through walls out to somewhere distant. Darren grunted as she squeezed out a bullet with a knot of the white threads wrapped around it. It clattered to the floor near a blackened piece of flesh close to the same size.

I had never seen these lights with Laura when she'd healed me. Surely I would have noticed.

The Knight staggered and started to take quicker breaths, but in moments his expression softened. I'd been so focused on surviving and keeping Tyler from exploding that I hadn't considered what Darren had gone through. I'd have to thank him at some point. I had a lot of people to thank, and a few debts to repay.

Benjamin was texting, and that made me a little nervous. I had the sense that I was waiting for Friday to finish healing Darren, so Tyler and I waited awkwardly one step from the floor. The pool of blood from the guard I'd split had finally stopped spreading. Gregor didn't seem to be bleeding at all.

We should let Deanna know Tyler is okay. What exactly would we tell her? "Where's your phone?" I asked Tyler.

"Dropped it at the house. I'm pretty sure. They drugged me, so I'm not one hundred percent sure."

Friday gave me a withering look and I stopped talking, watching the light show that fired under her fingertips.

Khimmer, do you see lights around Friday's hands?

No, Mistress.

Could Tyler see it? Benjamin? Darren? They didn't seem to be watching her.

She finished with Darren, and though he appeared to be in less pain, I thought he might sit down from exhaustion. Friday spun to study Tyler. "You don't appear to be injured." She gestured toward the front door. "Wait over there. We'll be leaving together." To me she pointed to the steps. "Sit."

I sighed, not even realizing until that moment that I wanted her to heal me. Nightarmor's stiff leg didn't make it easy, but I balanced on a higher step and grasped a balustrade with my right hand to steady myself. Friday crouched on the stairs and peered deeply into my eyes as if I'd smacked my head.

I was just about to explain where I was injured when she whispered, "When I give you a signal, replace the armor with your earlier costume."

My eyes flicked to Benjamin who still texted and then to Darren, partially obscured by the railing. I nodded imperceptibly to her.

Khimmer, on Friday's signal, remove armor, replace with earlier costume.

Yes, Mistress.

Friday loosened her collar, the lights streamed out in threads, and a small Samurai climbed out of her dress and hopped to the floor. I smiled as I recognized the outfit from one of Tyler's books. The armor was gray and realistic with scratches and a red gorget. The Samurai took two test strokes of its sword as it grew to full size. Short but squat, it blocked us from view. Friday mouthed, "Now."

Nightarmor flowed around me, and the cumbersome helmet was replaced with the silver and black mask on a stick. Without the compression Khimmer had kept on my flesh, my knee flared in pain. Purple and dark red mottled swollen skin, and the knee cap looked askew. I clamped my mouth tight to avoid crying out.

"I like to give them a good show. It came in handy this time," Friday said quietly. I barely noted the Samurai dropping to its smaller size, but I shivered when Fluffy scrambled off my back. Friday frowned as it hopped on one foot to her dress. "Seems you needed help," Friday said.

Nodding, I wasn't ready to trust myself speaking yet. Turben had never accepted my reactions to pain. "Sorry."

"Shh." She almost sounded comforting. Her tattoo skittered under her collar, and she reached for my hand and flipped it over. The spider spit light streaming into the air and rose from my skin. Friday spoke quiet enough that the others couldn't hear. "Glad we didn't need this."

I was as well. The possibility had gotten close. The spider crawled happily enough to settle in the blank patch in Friday's wrinkled skin. I couldn't look at my knee. Gregor's corpse had paled too quickly except for a dark rim around his eyes. The thought of the symbiont waiting inside it gave me the creeps. Darren and Tyler avoided each other, shifting awkwardly while shooting glances in my direction. Benjamin was still texting. I hoped we didn't end up with an army of angry Upre showing up. Somehow, I bet that Friday might be a match for them.

"It's going to get worse before it gets better." Friday rested her fingertips on my knee.

The moment she made contact I considered blacking out. If light wove from her fingers, I didn't see them with my eyes pressed closed. A few noises escaped my lips, and I did hear Tyler's frantic voice once. I hadn't realized I was gripping the balustrade until Tyler wrapped their hand around mine. Their presence gave me both some comfort and shame. They needed me to be strong.

When the pain subsided enough that I opened my eyes again, both Benjamin and Darren were gone. From under Friday's fingertips, light threaded out from my knee, some tying to Tyler or myself. Hunger gnawed at my nauseous stomach. My parched throat ached for something to drink.

"Getting close," she said. "You'll want to immobilize it with a brace. Keep off it. Reduce the swelling as much as you can." Her voice still had a brusque quality to it, but I could sense that she cared.

"Would you mind if we came to visit you again, someday?"

"Why do you hate me so much?" The corner of her lip twitched in a teasing smile. "Anytime. I'd like to learn more about you. You, I'm sure, could learn a thing or two from me."

"Like the lights?"

"Shush." She glanced toward the hall to the garage. I guessed that was where Darren and Benjamin had gone. "Keep it to yourself. Dangerous as your little friend if word gets out." Friday pulled her hands back, and the white threads vanished. "Hey, Tyler. She needs a shoulder to hang on, and it's not mine."

Pulling up on the railing, I kept my weight off the leg, though the pain was gone. My skin had a purple tinge to it, and the swelling puffed the knee slightly. "Thank you," I said. "For everything." Tyler hurried over, but she interrupted by handing me the black and silver square.

Tyler grabbed it. "Where's your phone?"

I was pulling the cell phone out when Darren walked from the hall, settling his hat on his head. He carried his jacket draped over his arm.

Benjamin followed close behind. "Hate to break up the party, but some family is coming around. Best I explain this alone."

Darren shook his head. "I'm staying." He raised a phone. "I've got to check in. I'll check in with you in a couple of days," he said to me.

Handing Tyler my phone, I drew a more relaxed breath than I'd taken in a day. "Thank you, for trying."

He snorted. "There's going to be a ton of questions the Knights will be asking. However, thank you. I wasn't sure why they were keeping me alive, or if they planned to have me bleed out on the floor." Darren tipped his hat. "I'll be in touch."

Benjamin nodded to my leg. "Sorry about everything, Ma'am. Won't be no more trouble from us."

Friday snorted. "I imagine some of Gregor's men haven't got the word. We'll want to be careful." She gestured to my mask.

"Can't guarantee it's all clear." He smiled and gestured to Gregor's body. "My men have gotten the message through to a couple of his; they're being mighty helpful now."

She motioned us toward the front door. I had one arm over Tyler's shoulder and hopped toward the entry. The reek of blood and spilled entrails weighed heavy in the air. I ached to step out that door into fresh air and sunshine. I could hear music outside.

Friday stepped to the door and turned to Benjamin. "You got this mess?"

"Yes, Ma'am."

CHAPTER 35

FRIDAY STEPPED DOWN THE STAIRS, and her yellow butterflies fluttered in from the right side of the yard. Behind my mask, I inhaled a deep breath of city air, and despite the exhaust, it smelled like freedom. Revelers meandered along the side street outside the iron gates. If possible, their costumes had become more colorful. One person walked on stilts like the jugglers at a market, except he wore clothes split down the middle with green on one side and red on the other. A bell jostled on his hat. Scents of baking bread and a tinge of alcohol floated in the breeze.

We walked outside the gates, and Friday motioned to the stone base of the iron fence. "Sit."

I glanced at all the people milling on the street and intersection. Cars tried to work their way past. "Is it safe?"

Friday's butterflies dropped behind her collar. "With Benjamin's people out here, yes. Possibly the safest spot." She studied Tyler. "You've got some abilities, minor empathy. You would have been trained if you were in the right family, or strong enough. Do you understand how important it is to keep this out of the media? Not to talk about this? I assume you do, or the Knights would have had a different response around you."

Tyler helped me sit on the stone block and adjusted the ridiculous cape to my side. "The more I see, yes. People would freak if they knew. They'd probably hunt you and all the others."

"They have, more than once. We manage to get a handle on it eventually. The Knights have been at this for thousands of years."

I leaned against the iron rails, happy to rest. "We need to get back to Tallahassee. Let Deanna know." Some food would be good, even something to drink. I felt stupid holding the mask.

Friday gestured toward my phone which Tyler held, along with the black and silver square. "Put the battery back. Get a ride and get out of New Orleans until we've made sure we've cleared up any orders Gregor might have out there."

Tyler pointed to the sidewalk. "Here?"

"I said it was the safest spot, didn't I?" Friday studied me before telling me her phone number.

I looked from her to my phone where Tyler had removed the back. *Do you have that number?* I thought to Khimmer.

Yes, Mistress.

"When should I call you?" I asked.

"When you're ready to learn. Rest up." Friday turned, checked the car approaching, and stepped off the curve as if to leave.

"Wait!" I almost tried to stand.

She turned. "Don't tell me you want a hug or something."

I did, but just said, "Thank you." I might not have survived without her.

I watched her walk away, weaving through the people until she disappeared around the brick building at the intersection. Friday seemed to have answers for me, but not for the questions I'd been asking. I would come back to New Orleans.

Tyler stood holding my phone and glancing up and down the street without focusing on anything in particular. Out in the sunlight away from the carnage inside, their clothes were rumpled and hair disheveled. "What's the story? I'm assuming Deanna has the police involved along with a team of detectives. Did she know you were coming here?"

I hadn't considered anything but getting home, and assumed we'd be flying. Deanna and Tyler flew everywhere. "Tell them you escaped." That wouldn't explain why I was here. Tyler would have to go home alone. "Go to the police here. Tell them you jumped out of the trunk like that story. The one with the red cover."

Tyler's lips tightened. "How does that explain you being here?"

"Doesn't. I'll . . ." I sighed. "I'll ask Darren to drive me." The Knight had to be going back at some point.

"No, I'm not leaving you here."

I reached my hand out for my phone. The longer we argued, the longer it would be before Deanna could stop worrying and Tyler could get somewhere safe. Safer. Earth no longer felt safe. "I'd love to hear your plan." I patted the stone beside me.

Tyler slumped down beside me, relinquishing the phone. I felt as tired as they looked. "I can't think."

"I'll be okay. It'll take a little while longer for me to get there." I let the mask rise off my face to speak. Friday had said it was safe here. Why did I need a disguise?

Tyler frowned and glanced around, as if searching for an answer. The sun had risen above the trees and buildings to our left. I'd love a shower.

I texted Darren, "Can I get a ride back with you?" Tilting the phone, I waited for Tyler to glance at it and frown harder.

"You're right. I can't take any chance of you being connected to this." Tyler placed their elbows on their knees and buried their face in their hands. "I'm lousy at lying."

"One of the reasons I love you." I rocked my shoulder into Tyler's and remembered the kiss. A flush rose up my cheeks. Relief came when my phone vibrated with a message from Darren.

"A woman is picking you up. B's. She'll get you to a room to wait for me." I assumed the B stood for Benjamin.

Tyler read the message. "So that's that. I hate this." They stood and stared at the branches above that dangled from Gregor's yard. "I'll call or message when I get back. Act surprised."

I was digging through my dull brain for a witty response when a gray sedan stopped in front of us. A dark-haired woman thumbed through an open window to the seat behind her. She glanced in her mirrors as if in a hurry. Tyler helped me up and got me to the door.

"I'll call," Tyler said once I was seated.

Under any other circumstance, I would have told them I loved them. The words almost came automatically, but the kiss had made things awkward. Tyler was just a friend. "Okay," I said.

We left Tyler standing partly in the road, with the car

behind us hurrying to get through the holiday throng. The woman drove me silently to a three-story mansion that had been turned into some sort of hostel. The man at the desk worked with her to get me up to the Shadows Room, which I found an intriguing name. There was a tub of some sort, but I focused on a basket of muffins and breads on the dresser and the tea he brought up for me before I fell back on the bed and crashed.

When I woke, it was dark outside, and Darren sat reading on a settee that reminded me of the Queen's palace in Vale Agnor. I had to pee. "Couldn't get your own room?" He had on fresh clothes, and I swore he'd showered.

Pain twinged my knee when I started to get off the bed. I could still smell the muffins and peered in to see if he'd eaten the brown one. He hadn't.

"Hold on." He retrieved a blue contraption from the seat next to him and threw it on the bed. "Put that on." It had dangling straps flopping off it as it bounced on the blanket. A white container of pills followed, then a bottle of water, and he slid the crutch beside it all as he stood.

I grabbed the crutch and hobbled for the bathroom. The tub was a strange shape and stood out from the wall. Someone had left a smiling yellow duck on the edge to watch me pee. I could use fresh clothes and a shower. It had been a long day, and I still hadn't shaken off the stress. I stood, flushed, and stared at the tub. "I'm taking a bath," I yelled. We had a long ride together; it was for his benefit as much as mine. He shouldn't complain.

Before I could work my way to the tub, Darren tapped on the door. "Fresh clothes."

I looked at the distance to the door. "Can you put them inside?"

He managed to open the door and place the brace and

clothes in a neat pile without making eye contact, though I hadn't undressed. He'd even bought a packaged set of underwear.

The bath felt wonderful. Human again, I left the hostel in the middle of the night with a snug brace and learning to navigate stairs with a crutch. Gregor had been stopped.

The air had a chilly bite to it. "Gregor, or the symbiont, what will happen?"

"We'll monitor the Upre once the symbiont takes a new host. The family is cooperative. They'd been waiting for Gregor to pass."

"So, it won't really be Gregor?"

"The human host meld will create a new personality, to a certain extent. That's why we'll monitor."

I didn't completely understand, but it didn't sound like I needed to worry about Gregor or an Upre vendetta. Maybe Laura could explain the symbiont/human/Upre connection better. As long as the Upre left me alone, I didn't really care. Tyler was free. I was heading home to Woo. The only consequences were a few debts I owed. Vivianne might have an idea what I could expect the high Fae to ask me. My stomach growled as we exited.

"Can we eat?"

"Waffle House, Slidell." Darren still favored his left arm as he opened the door to let me in his car. A thin plastic bag with pistachios and cans of tea were on the passenger floor. His car still smelled stale, but it was headed in the right direction.

Tyler's call came after our second gas station, when the sky ahead of us had just started to lighten into a dull gray.

CHAPTER 36

WHEN WE PULLED up to my house, I realized I'd forgotten to tell Laura I was coming back. Shadows still darkened my front yard, but I recognized Laura's car parked beside the flamingos. The local birds were calling out to the sun.

"Hades." I scrambled to get my harness off and reach back for my crutch.

Darren looked tired. I never asked if he'd gotten any sleep. We hadn't talked much during the drive; I didn't want to give him anything to question. He'd been tight-lipped about Friday.

"I'll see you around," I said. I'd stuffed my old clothes in a food bag along with snacks I hadn't finished.

Darren's eyebrows raised. "I'm assigned to you now, so yes."

I didn't ask what that entailed. "Thank you for helping."

The new neighbor had a light on behind curtains, but I saw no sign of him. My crutch inadvertently took out a Flamingo. Hobbling, I couldn't make it up the steps before Mrs. Forster came out of her door.

"What have you gotten into now?"

I hopped up another step and ignored her.

"There's a fine line between self-confidence and hubris." She timed each comment with a step. "You'll take risks not expecting any consequences. You'll end up hurting yourself or others. Take a look at what you pride yourself in and if you find no fault, you need to rein that in."

Laura opened my front door, rescuing me. "Are you okay?"

"Twisted knee," I lied.

She grabbed the bag in my fingers and bustled me inside, leaving Mrs. Forster's comments ignored. "Damn, Ahnjii." She closed the door. "You need a chair."

Woo whistled, turned pink, and climbed down from the cabinet above the kitchen window.

"I'll sit." I leaned against the wall by the door and slid down. "You won't believe all this." Woo climbed up my chest as I began telling my story, or at least a version that didn't include Nightarmor. I scratched Woo's fur while they nestled under my neck, before they decided to check my snack bag. I'd saved some pistachios.

Laura stopped me a couple of times for questions, mostly about Friday and her tattoo magic. She waved off heading to her studio when we realized what time it was.

"Tyler's free, and there is no Gregor anymore, just his symbiont. All that's good. But, do you really think the Upre families will leave you alone?" she asked.

I had, until she questioned it. I'd just gotten out of one vendetta with the wildlings. "You don't? Benjamin seemed pretty sure that what Gregor was doing broke some sort of rule of theirs."

"Oh, it did. The Knights are pretty insistent on a voluntary signing of contracts. The Upre have always honored it, much as we do."

"The Nedjir?"

Laura blinked, highlighting her cherry red eyes. "We didn't compel in the same way as the high Fae or Upre, but we used sigils to manipulate humans into serving us."

I found it hard to believe that people like Laura or the relatives I'd met would do that. "Friday said the Knights have been around for thousands of years."

"Yes. They're in all but the most ancient songs. We were nearly destroyed by their ancestors." She pointed to my leg. "So, are you going to relax a bit now?"

"I will, if people stop threatening my friends."

Woo whistled and meandered across the floor toward me.

"You, too, Woo." I let them crawl up onto my chest. "I won't let anyone come after you." I smiled with my friends nearby while I sat in my own apartment. I could sleep again. Tyler might be available for a visit this evening. Deanna was still on high alert, and the police were driving by regularly in case the kidnappers came back. We couldn't tell them Tyler was safe.

"I'm glad you're home safe." Laura rested her shoulder against mine.

"Me, too."

She tapped my knee lightly. "Want me to give it a try? I might be able to strengthen it a bit, especially since you've rested and eaten."

"It couldn't hurt." I smiled, but had another interest beyond fixing my knee.

When Laura healed, I didn't see any threads of light.

CHAPTER 37

I ate fresh-cooked noodles with Woo after Laura left. Tyler promised Pho soon, but Deanna wasn't letting them out of the house. After all the junk food from gas stations, my ramen tasted like savory perfection. The scent mixed with Woo's cinnamon deliciously.

Woo sat on the counter across from my bowl, delicately picking up the short strands I laid over the edge. I texted Tyler, "When is a good time to come over?"

"This evening. One of the detectives is coming over in an hour or so. I hate this."

I knew Tyler meant they didn't like lying. "I'll check in later, before I come over." With the crutch, it would take more time than usual. Maybe I'd get a ride with Laura.

Woo whistled a low lament when I left to visit Vivianne. "I'm coming back. Promise."

I couldn't escape Mrs. Forster completely, but I navigated the last few steps ignoring her. The flamingos were properly arranged in the dirt and sparse grass.

Vivianne opened the door to the bookstore and looked at my crutch. "Nails, what happened?"

As we maneuvered through the store to a chair, I explained while checking the room for coworkers. I could hear them in the back. I told her about Tyler's kiss.

"I knew it." Vivianne held three books in the crook of her arm. "You don't want to admit it, but the passion is there."

"It's not." I flicked the end of my braid. "I don't want it there, anyway." Just being friends with Tyler had nearly gotten them killed. "A thank you kiss, that's all."

"I never got a thank you kiss from you." She laughed, squeezing a book onto a shelf.

"Tyler had an explosive around their neck."

"Maybe you're right, but you're the one who mentioned the kiss." She waved a finger at me as if scolding me. "It's on *your* mind."

When I backtracked to meeting the Council, Vivianne shoved books at the edge of a shelf and sat in a chair. I had a dark calico in my lap. "I got Gregor's city out of them, but I owe them a debt."

Her ears twitched. "You're an idiot."

I thought of Friday. "You're not the first to tell me. Too late. If I hadn't had that information, Darren might not have taken me to New Orleans."

"You can't know what they'll ask you to do. Always negotiate the price with the high Fae first, you know that."

I didn't. I wasn't an Earth witch and hadn't had family to train me. I just bumbled along the best I could. "I was desperate." I couldn't tell Vivianne that the high Fae might not have let me leave with Nightarmor. "Yes, I was an idiot."

By the time I hobbled for the door, I'd learned new Fae curses. Vivianne propped the door open for me and kept a gray tabby from attempting an escape. "Drop by tomorrow?"

"I will, love you." I reached the screen door. "Hades."

Idin waited for me at the bottom of the steps.

Vivianne coughed. "Bye."

The inner door closed behind me as I stepped onto the porch. The morning had warmed, and the shrubs planted around the building smelled alive. Idin looked out of place in Railroad Square with his nubs, tall Fae ears, and blood-red hair.

He scowled as I made my way slowly down the steps. "The Council wants a report on Gregor."

"I don't work for the Council." I smiled. "However, I could consider the report a payment of my debt." It wouldn't work, but it would make Idin angry.

He fumed, barely making room for me to get off the steps. "No. They expect a report."

I studied his angry face. "I'm in no mood to hobble off to your tree and then down through the forest."

"Report to me."

My ears warmed. Idin, despite being Shailagh's boss, acted as little more than an escort for the Council. "No. I'll tell my story to Shailagh."

He grunted and crossed his arms. "She's on other duties."

I shrugged and headed for the end of Railroad Square where the Crum Box and the Square Mug Café waited. There was no reason to go in that direction, except to get away from Idin.

He easily caught up with me. "Shailagh's not available; you'll have to report to me."

"Shailagh or no report. You choose." I imagined the Council would not appreciate either option, but the latter less so. Two steps later, I felt the light vibration that I recognized as the high Fae sigil magic they used to communicate. "I'll be at the Crum Box," I called over my shoulder. Pete's mac and cheese was the best. I could squeeze in a little.

I'd long since finished my snack when Shailagh arrived with Idin. Her expression was unreadable. Did she regret betraying me? My crutch leaned against the bench on my side of the weathered table, so I motioned to the bench on the opposite side. They both looked at the metal canopy above but didn't seem affected by it.

Before she sat, Shailagh tapped her ear lobe. "You can get rid of that. I won't use the other one anymore."

My throat thickened. "You betrayed me."

"Yes." Shailagh sat nearly on the center of the bench. "Which is why I got rid of the pairing piece. They can do their own work." Her face remained expressionless. "I didn't expect to see you again."

Idin remained standing behind her. Anger flickered in his eyes, and his frown tightened.

I still wanted to be her friend. They'd forced her to betray me, and she'd reacted by getting rid of the ability to do so ever again. I could admire that. "Sorry. I'll only speak with you from now on. Grumpy is welcome to tag along if he wants, but if the Council has a message, it comes through you."

I swore the bushes behind me rustled. Shailagh's lips lifted on one side, short of a smile. "Understood. Tyler is back. What happened to Gregor?"

"Dead. The host that is. I sort of blew him up. I was planning on shoving a blade through host and symbiont, but it didn't work out that way." I grinned. "Met a new friend. She's cool."

CHAPTER 38

THE SUN HAD SETTLED to a comfortable place near the horizon by the time Laura dropped me off at Tyler and Deanna's house. The long shadows had already begun to chill the air. The kids were still loud at the daycare.

Deanna met me at the door, phone to her ear. "No. She's a friend." She nodded for me to enter. "Thank you." The house smelled like curry, and hunger tugged at my stomach. She lowered the phone with a laugh. "They warned me you were coming. It doesn't look like you could be a threat if you wanted to be. Tyler said you twisted your knee. No skating for a while."

I hadn't noticed anyone outside. *Khimmer, was someone outside watching?*

One car drove by when you were let out, Mistress.

"Where's Tyler?"

"Cooking. I'm so happy they're safe. Sorry I won't let them out to play."

I knew Tyler obliged Deanna's kidnapping concerns and wished that I could let her know it was over. "That's okay, I'd rather they stay safe."

John peered at my crutches as we walked into the room where he watched television. "Need to be more careful." He still wore a brace from when I'd hurt him, but he didn't remember how he got hurt.

"Accidents happen." I liked the phrase, especially when I didn't want to actually talk about a situation.

We ate together, the four of us. Tyler and I tried to keep Deanna from harping on the kidnapping while John made sour comments. It made enjoying Tyler's sumptuous dinner difficult. I was happy when we finally headed up to Tyler's room. The night made it too chilly to hang at the pool. Deanna and John moved back to her cats and their television.

I rested my crutch on the side of Tyler's bed and sat. "I was scared." The emotion hadn't really controlled me during the skirmish, but the fear of losing Tyler had been present since the kidnapping. Before I reached the house, I planned on telling Tyler most of what had transpired.

"Me too. I can get pretty valiant when I'm on a crusade for someone else, but I thought I'd piss myself a couple of times there. In the end, I was more afraid they'd hurt you. I knew you'd come looking for me." Tyler's eyes looked dark, as if from lack of sleep more than makeup. They touched their neck where the explosive had been. "Thought I'd lose my head at one point." They smiled and grabbed a book off their desk.

I couldn't imagine what I would have done if it had gone badly. Another reason Turben and the Aegis monks proscribed relationships. "Did you sleep?" I asked.

"Not really. Naps." Tyler tossed a book onto the bed with a young woman on the cover.

"What's this?"

"Jane Austen," Tyler replied as they sat. "You need to start your own book collection. Tell me if you like it."

"I can get books at Vivianne's."

Tyler tucked their knees up and leaned into the pillows. "Consider it a thank you or Valentine's Day gift."

Khimmer?

Unknown, Mistress. I assume it's a holiday named after someone called Valentine, a birthday perhaps?

With Tyler, I didn't have to hide my ignorance. "Who's Valentine?" Earth had a lot of holidays.

"There's a number of stories, but I like the saint who got his head lopped off for marrying people against an emperor's wishes. Sort of romantic."

I blushed, thinking of our kiss. "I'm glad you're safe."

"I didn't like you risking yourself."

I'd do it all over again.

Please head to my website and join my mailing list if you'd like to be kept up to date on this series or my other books.

Khimmer Chronicles

Wight's Wrath - Book One

Death's Contract - Book Two

Fate's Betrayal - Book Three

High Fae's Quest - Book Four

Friday's Fifth - Book Five

If you haven't read the Origin story of the **AngelSong** series, *Shattered Blood,* then download a free ebook or purchase the paperback or audible on Amazon.

AngelSong Series

Penumbra - Book One

Red Tempest - Book Two

Coerced - Book Three

Demons' Lair - Book Four

Infrared - Book Five. (End of the AngelSong Series)

Website KevinArthurDavis.com

Facebook @KevinArthurDavis

KevinADavis on Instagram

KevinADavisUF on Twitter

ACKNOWLEDGMENTS

April appears to like Ahnjii.

Robyn Huss, my editor, is amazing and I consider her work an art form. She transforms my worst into my best.

October K Santerelli works wonders with a detailed sensitivity read. Check out his novels and I highly recommend his services.

I receive wonderful support from Katharine, Mark, Rosemary, Tim, and Vail from our JordanCon writing group (the infamous Fireside Group), Dianne and Brett from our Apex brainstorming group, and Arrash and Michele from Jody Lynn Nye's DragonCon workshop.

I mourn the loss of David Farland's tireless and caring mentorship. Pick up one of his books for the magic he endowed. Writers, study his lessons at Apex Writers.

Jody Lynn Nye's DragonCon workshop taught me how to use critiques.

The spectacular cover art is by Rebekah at VividCovers! Consider her for your next design.

Thank you.